Uniquely Us: The Beauty of Our Differences

Diversity and Inclusion

Victoria Bennett

Published by The Good Child Bookstore, 2024.

UNIQUELY US: THE BEAUTY OF OUR DIFFERENCES

First edition. October 26, 2024.

ISBN: 979-8227961297

Written by Victoria Bennett.

Table of Contents

Dedication

To every child who has ever felt different—this book is for you. May you always know that your uniqueness is your greatest strength, and that the world is a more beautiful place because you are in it. To the dreamers, the explorers, the quiet thinkers, and the loud adventurers—embrace who you are, because there is only one you. And to the parents, teachers, and caregivers who nurture this spirit of acceptance, thank you for showing children that our differences are what make us extraordinary. Keep celebrating diversity, for it is the key to a kinder, more magical world.

Preface

The inspiration behind "Uniquely Us: The Beauty of Our Differences" came from a desire to share an important truth with children: that being different is not only okay, but it's what makes life vibrant and exciting. Throughout this story, you will meet characters of all shapes, sizes, and backgrounds, each with their own unique abilities and challenges. They face incredible adventures, learn from one another, and grow in their understanding of themselves and the world around them.

As a writer, I wanted to create a magical, diverse world where every child could see themselves, whether they are the quiet observer, the fearless adventurer, or somewhere in between. My hope is that this book not only entertains but also sparks conversations about the beauty of diversity, acceptance, and kindness. Let this journey remind us all that our differences, when embraced, create a symphony that makes the world a better place.

Chapter 1: The Gathering at Harmony Hill

A gentle breeze swept across the vast fields of golden flowers as the sun dipped below the horizon, painting the sky in hues of pink, orange, and lavender. Harmony Hill had always been a place of wonder, a place whispered about in the legends of old. Some said it was the meeting point of the stars and the earth, where magic filled the air and impossible things happened. But for most, Harmony Hill was simply a dream, a place they would never see or touch. Until now.

In the heart of this legendary place, a strange occurrence began to unfold. From distant corners of the world, from towns hidden behind mountains and villages perched on cliffs, from forests deep and oceans wide, a select few received their invitations.

Ellie was the first to notice hers. She was a young girl from the seaside town of Marindale, her curly brown hair often tangled in the sea breeze, and her eyes the color of the ocean depths. Ellie had always felt a little different. She could hear the whispers of the sea, the quiet songs of the waves as they kissed the shore. One afternoon, as she strolled by the water, a peculiar conch shell washed up at her feet. Inside the shell, a small note was tucked away, its ink glowing faintly. "You are invited to Harmony Hill," it read.

From the forest village of Silverbark came Lila, a girl with skin like the bark of trees and hair as green as leaves in the spring. Lila was known for her deep connection to the forest, where she could communicate with animals and plants alike. One morning, while she sat by a creek, a squirrel approached her with a tiny scroll tied to its tail. The message, though short, was clear: "Your presence is requested at Harmony Hill."

Meanwhile, across the distant mountains, a boy named Rafi received his own invitation. Rafi was unlike anyone else in his village. Born with wings that shimmered in the sunlight like those of a dragonfly, he had always struggled to fit in. On the night of a full moon, while practicing his flying near the cliffs, a glowing firefly hovered in front of him. It blinked three times and then morphed into a scroll, which read, "Harmony Hill awaits you."

But it wasn't just humans who were called to Harmony Hill. Creatures from myths and legends also felt the pull. In the enchanted caves beneath the ocean, a young mermaid named Coralia found a pearl in her underwater garden. When she touched it, the pearl broke open, revealing a map that led to Harmony Hill.

In the cloud kingdom of Aerion, Zephyr, a creature with the body of a lion and the wings of an eagle, received a visit from the wind itself. It whispered in his ear, "You are needed at Harmony Hill." Zephyr had always felt like he didn't quite belong in the sky or on the ground, and the promise of a place like Harmony Hill intrigued him.

One by one, each child and creature set out on their journey, guided by their unique invitations. Harmony Hill, once a distant legend, was becoming real. The path to Harmony Hill was not straightforward, however. For Ellie, it involved crossing vast oceans, guided by the stars and the whispers of the sea. Lila had to journey through dense forests, communicating with trees that shared ancient secrets of the land. Rafi, flying through the skies, dodged storms and soaring over valleys until he saw the glow of Harmony Hill in the distance.

For Coralia, the journey was beneath the waves, through shimmering coral forests and past ancient shipwrecks, until the water seemed to grow lighter and brighter. As for Zephyr, his flight through the skies was filled with strange, magical clouds, each one testing his resolve and courage in different ways.

At last, they arrived. Harmony Hill was not what they had expected. It was simple, a rolling hill covered in wildflowers, but the air shimmered with magic, and the sky above seemed wider, deeper, more filled with possibilities than anywhere else. Each character stepped onto the hill, and though they had never met before, they felt an instant connection. It was as though the hill itself whispered to them, telling them they belonged.

Ellie was the first to speak, her voice soft but filled with wonder. "I've heard about this place in stories. But I never thought it was real."

"It feels like we're meant to be here," Lila added, her fingers brushing the petals of a flower that seemed to bloom brighter at her touch.

Rafi, who had landed quietly beside them, folded his wings and nodded. "I've felt out of place everywhere I've been. But here... it's different."

Coralia swam in a nearby lake that seemed to appear just for her. "The water here sings," she said, her voice like the gentle bubbling of a stream.

Zephyr, towering over the group with his majestic wings, looked down at the others. "This hill holds more power than I've ever felt in the clouds," he rumbled. "But why were we called here?"

Before anyone could answer, a soft, glowing light began to form in the center of the hill. It swirled and shifted, growing larger until it formed the shape of an old man, his beard made of starlight and his eyes glowing like the moon. "Welcome to Harmony Hill," the figure said, his voice deep and soothing. "You have all been chosen because you are different. And it is in those differences that the future of our world depends."

The group looked at one another, confused but curious.

"You have each been brought here because there is a task only you can accomplish," the figure continued. "The world is vast and filled with many kinds of people and creatures. But not all understand the beauty of diversity. It is up to you to teach them."

"Teach them what?" Ellie asked, her voice quivering slightly.

"Teach them that our differences make us stronger," the figure replied. "That every being, no matter how different, has a place in the world."

Lessons Learned

1. **Difference is beautiful** – each character's unique qualities led them to Harmony Hill.
2. **Belonging comes from within** – they all felt out of place in their own worlds but found a connection on the hill.
3. **Nature speaks in many ways** – through the ocean, the trees, and even the stars, guiding each character.
4. **Diversity strengthens us** – the group is stronger together because of their differences.
5. **Curiosity opens doors** – each character's willingness to follow their invitation brought them to a magical place.
6. **Magic exists in the unexpected** – Harmony Hill, a place of legends, became real for those who believed.
7. **Teamwork begins with connection** – the group felt a bond as soon as they arrived, even though they had never met.
8. **Listening to the world reveals hidden paths** – from animals to waves, nature's signs helped guide them.
9. **Purpose is discovered through unity** – they were brought together to teach others the value of diversity.
10. **Courage is stepping into the unknown** – despite not knowing what awaited, they all embarked on the journey.

Chapter 2: The Great Puzzle of Connection

The first night at Harmony Hill was unlike any the group had experienced before. The stars above seemed to hum with an ancient melody, and the air itself felt alive with possibility. As they sat around a small fire that Lila had conjured from the branches of a nearby tree, the group reflected on the mysterious figure's words.

"What do you think he meant?" Rafi asked, stretching his wings out behind him. "That we're supposed to teach people about being different?"

"I don't know," Ellie replied, her voice thoughtful. "But it feels like there's something bigger going on here."

Before they could continue the conversation, a low rumble echoed through the hill. The ground beneath them trembled slightly, and the air became thick with anticipation. Suddenly, a large, glowing structure began to rise from the center of the hill. It was made of stone and glass, twisting and turning into a complex, intricate shape that seemed to change every time they blinked.

"What is that?" Coralia asked, her wide eyes reflecting the glow of the strange structure.

The group stood and cautiously approached it. As they neared, they could see that the structure was not just a random collection of shapes. It was a puzzle, and it was missing pieces.

"I think we're supposed to solve it," Zephyr said, his deep voice echoing slightly in the stillness of the night.

"But how?" Lila asked, staring up at the massive structure that towered over them.

"It looks like the pieces are scattered around the hill," Ellie observed, pointing to the faint glow of several puzzle pieces lying on the grass.

They each picked up a piece, examining it closely. The pieces were all different shapes and sizes, and each one seemed to reflect the character holding it. Ellie's piece was shaped like a wave, shimmering with the colors of the ocean. Lila's was shaped like a leaf, green and vibrant. Rafi's piece looked like a tiny pair of wings, Coralia's was a smooth, blue stone like the depths of the sea, and Zephyr's piece resembled a cloud.

"It's like the puzzle is connected to us," Ellie said softly.

"But how do we put it together?" Rafi asked, turning his piece over in his hands. "These pieces don't look like they fit."

"Maybe that's the point," Zephyr said thoughtfully. "We're all different. Maybe the puzzle isn't supposed to fit perfectly. Maybe we have to figure out how to connect our differences."

The group fell silent, contemplating Zephyr's words. It made sense. The mysterious figure had said they were brought here because of their differences. Perhaps this puzzle was a way of teaching them how to work together, even when they didn't seem to fit.

"I think we need to find more pieces," Lila said, glancing around the hill. "There must be others hidden here."

They spread out across Harmony Hill, searching for the remaining pieces of the puzzle. As they gathered them, they realized that each piece was as unique as they were. Some were smooth, others rough. Some were bright, while others were dull. But no matter how different they looked, each piece held a quiet power, as if it was waiting to reveal its place in the larger picture.

Once they had collected all the pieces, they returned to the glowing structure. The puzzle seemed even more complex up close, its shifting shapes reflecting the stars above.

"Now what?" Rafi asked, looking at the scattered pieces.

"We try," Zephyr said simply. "One piece at a time."

They began to fit the pieces together, but it wasn't easy. Some pieces seemed to repel each other, while others clicked into place only to fall apart moments later. Frustration began to creep in as the night wore on, but they refused to give up.

"Maybe we're going about this the wrong way," Ellie said after another failed attempt. "We're trying to force the pieces to fit. Maybe we need to let them guide us."

Lila nodded in agreement. "It's like the trees," she said. "When you listen to them, they show you the way. Maybe we need to listen to the puzzle."

They stood back and looked at the scattered pieces again, this time with a new perspective. Instead of trying to make them fit, they began to notice the subtle ways the pieces spoke to them. Ellie's wave-shaped piece seemed to flow toward Coralia's smooth, blue stone. Lila's leaf-like piece naturally curved toward Rafi's wing-shaped piece. Slowly but surely, the puzzle began to come together.

As the final piece clicked into place, the puzzle glowed brightly, illuminating the hill in a brilliant light. The structure twisted and shifted one last time before settling into a perfect shape. It was a representation of all of them—a tree with roots in the ocean, branches in the sky, and leaves that shimmered with the colors of the sea and the forest.

The group stood in awe of what they had created. It was a reminder that, no matter how different they were, they were all connected.

Lessons Learned

1. **Communication is key** – they had to learn how to communicate with each other and the puzzle.
2. **Patience leads to progress** – rushing the puzzle didn't work; they had to be patient.
3. **Collaboration strengthens the outcome** – by working together, they created something beautiful.
4. **Embrace differences** – the puzzle only came together because of the unique pieces.
5. **Listening brings understanding** – they had to listen to the puzzle and each other to solve it.

6. **Don't force things** – when they stopped forcing the pieces, the puzzle began to fit.
7. **Every piece has a place** – each piece of the puzzle, like each person, has a unique place.
8. **Trial and error is part of learning** – they made mistakes, but each one brought them closer to the solution.
9. **Connection is deeper than appearance** – the puzzle's pieces connected because of their deeper meanings.
10. **Unity through diversity** – the puzzle was a reflection of their unity, despite their differences.

Chapter 3: The Colors of the Sky

The morning after solving the great puzzle, the group awoke to a sky that was unlike any they had ever seen before. It was as if the sky itself was alive, shifting colors with every breath they took. Hues of pink, orange, and gold swirled above them, changing with every emotion they felt.

"I've never seen anything like this," Lila said in awe, her green hair glowing slightly in the sunlight.

"It's like the sky is connected to us," Ellie observed, her eyes wide with wonder.

Rafi stretched his wings and took to the air, flying high above the group. "You're right," he called down. "The higher I go, the more the colors change. It's like the sky is responding to what we feel."

Zephyr, ever the practical one, looked around. "This must be a sign. There's something more here for us to discover."

The group set off toward a village they had spotted in the distance. As they approached, they noticed that the village was unlike any they had seen before. The houses were small and simple, but the air around them shimmered with a vibrant energy. The villagers themselves were dressed in clothes that reflected the colors of the sky, each person surrounded by a faint glow.

"Welcome to the Festival of Colors," a villager said, greeting them with a warm smile. "You have arrived just in time."

"What is the Festival of Colors?" Coralia asked, her tail flicking slightly in excitement.

"It is a celebration of our emotions, our traditions, and the beauty of diversity," the villager explained. "The sky above us reflects our feelings, our joys, and our sorrows. It is a living canvas, and today, we invite you to add your own colors to it."

The group looked at each other, intrigued.

"How do we do that?" Lila asked.

The villager smiled and gestured to a large, open space in the center of the village. "Each of you has your own traditions, your own ways of expressing yourselves. Share those with us, and the sky will change to reflect your unique contributions."

Excitement buzzed through the group as they prepared to share their traditions. Ellie went first, walking to the center of the space with a seashell in hand. She raised it to her lips and blew a soft, melodic note. The sound echoed through the village, and as it did, the sky shifted to a deep, oceanic blue.

"This is a song from my village," Ellie explained, her voice soft but proud. "It's a song we play when we want to honor the sea and all the life it gives us."

The villagers clapped in appreciation, and Ellie's blue remained in the sky, swirling gently with the other colors.

Next, Lila stepped forward. She closed her eyes and began to hum, her voice growing louder as the ground beneath her feet began to tremble. Slowly, flowers began to bloom around her, their petals glowing with a soft, green light. As the flowers bloomed, the sky turned a rich, forest green.

"In my village, we sing to the trees and the earth," Lila explained, her eyes glowing with pride. "We believe that the earth listens to us, and we must honor it with our voices."

The villagers clapped once again, and Lila's green joined Ellie's blue in the sky.

Rafi was next. He leaped into the air, flying high above the village before diving down in a graceful arc. As he flew, the sky shifted to a bright, golden yellow, like the sunlight reflecting off his wings.

"In my village, we celebrate the freedom of flight," Rafi called out, his voice carried by the wind. "We believe that the sky is a place of endless possibilities, and we honor it with our flight."

The villagers cheered, and Rafi's golden yellow joined the other colors in the sky.

Coralia followed, diving into a nearby stream and sending ripples of blue and silver through the water. As she swam, the sky shifted to a soft, shimmering silver, like the light of the moon on the ocean.

"In my world, we honor the water," Coralia said, her voice echoing through the stream. "We believe that the water holds the secrets of the world, and we must protect it."

The villagers applauded, and Coralia's silver joined the other colors.

Finally, Zephyr stepped forward. He spread his massive wings and let out a powerful roar that echoed through the village. As he did, the sky shifted to a deep, stormy gray, like the clouds before a thunderstorm.

"In my kingdom, we honor the storms," Zephyr said, his voice deep and commanding. "We believe that the storms are a reminder of the power of nature and the balance between chaos and calm."

The villagers erupted into cheers, and Zephyr's stormy gray joined the vibrant colors in the sky.

As the group looked up, they marveled at the sky above them. It was a swirling canvas of blue, green, yellow, silver, and gray, each color representing their unique traditions and ways of life.

"You have all added your own colors to our sky," the villager said, smiling warmly. "And in doing so, you have made it more beautiful than ever."

The group stood together, feeling a deep sense of connection not only to each other but to the world around them. They had shared their differences, and in doing so, they had created something truly magical.

Lessons Learned

1. **Diversity adds beauty** – the sky became more beautiful with each unique contribution.
2. **Traditions are powerful** – each character's traditions held deep meaning and were honored by the villagers.
3. **Emotional expression is important** – the sky reflected their

emotions and traditions, showing the power of expression.

4. **Unity through individuality** – each color represented a different individual, but together, they created something unified.
5. **Celebration of differences** – the Festival of Colors was a celebration of the diversity that makes the world beautiful.
6. **Nature reflects our emotions** – the sky changed with their feelings, showing the deep connection between nature and emotions.
7. **Pride in one's heritage** – each character was proud of their traditions and shared them with joy.
8. **Collaboration enhances the world** – by sharing their traditions, they made the sky more vibrant.
9. **Cultural exchange enriches lives** – the villagers appreciated the group's traditions and were enriched by their stories.
10. **Harmony through diversity** – the sky was a perfect representation of harmony created through differences.

Chapter 4: In the Land of Giants and Fairies

The path from the village of the Festival of Colors led the group into an entirely new landscape. Gone were the vibrant skies and cheering villagers. In their place was a thick, dense mist that clung to the air, making it hard to see more than a few steps ahead. The trees here were tall, their trunks impossibly wide, and their branches stretched high into the sky, disappearing into the mist.

"Where are we now?" Coralia asked, her voice muffled by the fog.

"I'm not sure," Lila replied, her green hair damp from the moisture in the air. "But it feels... different."

Zephyr, ever vigilant, flapped his wings to clear the air around them, but the mist seemed to cling stubbornly to the ground. "We should be cautious," he warned. "This place is unlike any we've been before."

As they ventured deeper into the forest, they began to notice something strange. The trees, already massive, seemed to be growing even larger. The ground beneath their feet felt uneven, as though they were walking across a landscape that was shifting and changing with every step.

"I feel like I'm getting smaller," Rafi said, looking around in confusion. "Or maybe the trees are getting bigger?"

Ellie, who had been walking beside him, looked up. "It's not just the trees. Everything is getting bigger."

Before they could fully process what was happening, the group found themselves standing at the base of a tree that towered above them, its roots twisting and coiling around them like giant serpents.

"We're shrinking," Lila said in disbelief, her voice small and distant. "We're becoming... tiny."

Sure enough, the group had shrunk to the size of insects. The world around them, once familiar, had become enormous. The grass blades were as tall as trees, and the leaves above them were the size of rooftops.

"This is impossible," Rafi muttered, his wings fluttering in agitation.

"Not impossible," Zephyr said, his voice calm. "Just different."

As they adjusted to their new size, they noticed something even more peculiar. Creatures, small and delicate, flitted through the air around them. At first, they thought they were insects, but as the creatures came closer, they realized they were tiny fairies, their wings shimmering in the light.

"Welcome to the Land of Giants and Fairies," a small voice said, and the group turned to see a fairy with wings as delicate as butterfly wings hovering before them. "You are not the first to find yourself lost here."

"Where are we?" Ellie asked, her voice filled with wonder.

"You are in a place where size is only a matter of perspective," the fairy explained. "Here, the world shifts and changes depending on how you see it."

"How do we get back to normal size?" Coralia asked, looking around in confusion.

The fairy smiled. "That depends. You must first understand that size is relative. In this land, what is small can be large, and what is large can be small. It is all about how you choose to see the world."

As the group continued to explore the Land of Giants and Fairies, they began to realize that their size was not fixed. At times, they would grow taller, towering over the landscape like giants. Other times, they would shrink down to the size of ants, navigating a world that was both familiar and strange.

The lesson they learned in this land was one of perspective. They came to understand that size and power were not always the same. Sometimes, the smallest among them had the most significant impact. At other times, being larger didn't mean being stronger or more important.

Ellie, who had always felt small and insignificant compared to the vast ocean she loved, began to see that her size didn't define her. She realized that even though she was small, she could still make waves in the world.

Rafi, whose wings made him feel powerful, discovered that flight wasn't about size but about freedom. No matter how big or small he became, he could always soar.

Coralia, who lived in the depths of the ocean, learned that even the smallest ripple could create a wave that traveled far beyond what she could see.

And Zephyr, who was the largest and strongest of them all, came to understand that sometimes the greatest strength came from those who appeared the smallest and weakest.

In the Land of Giants and Fairies, they discovered that perspective was everything. They learned to see the world from different angles, to appreciate the small and the large, the weak and the strong, and to understand that every size had its place and purpose.

Lessons Learned

1. **Size is relative** – what seems small can be powerful, and what seems large can be fragile.
2. **Perspective changes everything** – how you see the world affects how you experience it.
3. **Strength comes in all sizes** – being big doesn't always mean being strong, and being small doesn't mean being weak.
4. **Small actions have big impacts** – even the tiniest ripple can create a wave.
5. **Growth is a process** – small things can grow into something magnificent over time.
6. **Power is not defined by appearance** – sometimes, the most powerful forces are the ones we overlook.
7. **Freedom comes from within** – no matter your size, you can

still find freedom.

8. **Every size has its place** – in the Land of Giants and Fairies, there was value in being both big and small.
9. **Adapting to change** – the group had to adapt to their shifting size and learn to navigate a changing world.
10. **Seeing from different angles** – by seeing the world from different sizes, they learned to appreciate all perspectives.

Chapter 5: Songs of the Wind

The path from the Land of Giants and Fairies led the group to a wide, open plain where the wind was the dominant force. It blew constantly, sometimes as a gentle breeze, sometimes as a powerful gust, but always carrying with it the sounds of music. The air was filled with melodies, soft and sweet, that seemed to come from nowhere and everywhere all at once.

"Where is that music coming from?" Ellie asked, her voice barely audible over the sound of the wind.

"It's the wind," Lila replied, her eyes closed as she listened. "It's singing."

The group paused, listening to the strange and beautiful music that filled the air. The wind carried with it not just sound but emotion—joy, sadness, excitement, and calm all woven together in a symphony that seemed to touch their very souls.

As they walked deeper into the plain, they noticed something unusual. The wind wasn't just carrying random music. It was responding to them, changing its tune based on their thoughts and feelings.

"It's like the wind knows what we're thinking," Coralia said, her voice filled with wonder.

"It does," a voice said, and the group turned to see an old man standing before them. His hair was wild and white, and his clothes billowed in the wind as if they were made of air itself.

"Who are you?" Zephyr asked, his wings shifting uneasily in the strong breeze.

"I am the Keeper of the Wind," the old man replied with a smile. "And you are standing in the land where music is the language of the soul."

"The wind is alive?" Rafi asked, his eyes wide with wonder.

The old man nodded. "In this land, the wind is not just a force of nature. It is a living thing, and it speaks to those who listen."

"But why does it change with our thoughts?" Ellie asked.

"Because the wind reflects your soul," the Keeper of the Wind explained. "It sings your feelings, your desires, your fears. It is the voice of your heart."

The group was silent for a moment, taking in the gravity of the old man's words. They had always known that the wind was powerful, but they had never imagined it could be so personal, so connected to their inner selves.

"Can we learn to sing with the wind?" Lila asked, her voice filled with excitement.

The Keeper of the Wind smiled. "Yes, but it is not something that can be taught. You must listen to the wind, feel its music in your heart, and let it guide you."

The group spent the rest of the day learning to listen to the wind. At first, it was difficult. The music seemed too complex, too elusive, like trying to catch smoke with their hands. But gradually, as they quieted their minds and opened their hearts, they began to hear the wind's song more clearly.

Ellie, with her deep connection to the ocean, was the first to understand. She closed her eyes and let the wind carry her thoughts, her hopes, and her dreams. The wind responded with a soft, gentle melody that reminded her of the waves lapping at the shore.

Lila was next. She sat on the ground, her hands resting on the earth, and listened to the wind as it rustled through the trees. The wind sang a song of growth and renewal, a song that spoke to the deep connection between the earth and the sky.

Rafi, ever the adventurer, leaped into the air, his wings catching the wind as he flew high above the plain. The wind responded with a joyous, soaring melody that filled him with a sense of freedom and possibility.

Coralia, always connected to the water, listened as the wind sang of the rivers and streams, of the water that flowed through the earth and the air. The wind's song was calm and steady, like the ebb and flow of the tides.

Finally, Zephyr, the largest and strongest of them all, stood still and let the wind swirl around him. The wind's song was deep and powerful, like the roar of a thunderstorm, but beneath the surface, there was a quiet strength, a reminder that even the fiercest storm had a heart of calm.

As the day turned to night, the group gathered together, their hearts filled with the music of the wind. They had learned that the wind was more than just a force of nature. It was a reflection of their souls, a language that spoke to their deepest selves.

The Keeper of the Wind watched them with a smile. "You have learned well," he said. "But remember, the wind is always changing, just as you are. Its song will be different tomorrow, and the day after that. But as long as you listen with your heart, you will always understand its music."

Lessons Learned

1. **The wind reflects the soul** – it carries the emotions and thoughts of those who listen.
2. **Music is a universal language** – the wind's song spoke to each character in a way they could understand.
3. **Listening is key to understanding** – by quieting their minds, they were able to hear the wind's song.
4. **Connection to nature** – the wind, like the ocean and the earth, is deeply connected to the natural world.
5. **Embrace change** – the wind is always changing, just as they are, and they must learn to adapt.
6. **Inner strength is quiet** – even the fiercest storm has a heart of calm, just as they do.

7. **Freedom comes from within** – the wind's song reminded them of the freedom they carry in their hearts.
8. **Emotions are powerful** – the wind's music was a reflection of their deepest emotions, showing the power of feeling.
9. **Harmony through diversity** – each character's connection to the wind was unique, but together, they created a harmonious melody.
10. **The journey is ongoing** – the wind's song will change, and so will they, but the journey of understanding continues.

Chapter 6: The Dance of Shadows and Light

The group had never seen a world quite like this one. As they stepped through a shimmering portal at the edge of the plain, they found themselves standing in a place where light and shadow intertwined in a perpetual dance. The land was neither dark nor bright, but a swirling mixture of both, where every beam of light cast an equally vivid shadow, and every shadow held a faint glimmer of light within it. The air itself seemed to hum with a quiet, almost sacred energy, as if this was a place where balance was of utmost importance.

Ellie, Rafi, Lila, Zephyr, and Coralia paused to take in the strange beauty of their surroundings. The ground beneath their feet shifted between bright patches of sunlight and deep pools of shadow with every step they took. It was as if the world itself was constantly in flux, never quite settling on one state or the other.

"Where are we?" Coralia asked, her voice soft as though speaking too loudly might disrupt the delicate balance of the place.

Zephyr narrowed his eyes, his powerful frame standing still as he studied the landscape. "This is a place of contrasts," he said. "A land of light and shadow. We must be careful here. Everything feels... fragile."

As the group continued their exploration, they noticed figures moving in the distance—strange beings made entirely of light and shadow. Some figures appeared almost human, while others were more abstract, their forms constantly shifting between darkness and light. These beings seemed to glide across the ground in pairs, always moving together in perfect harmony, as though engaged in a silent dance.

"Look at them," Lila whispered. "It's like they're dancing with each other."

"It's beautiful," Ellie added, her eyes wide with wonder. "But also a little eerie."

The group approached the figures cautiously, unsure of what to expect. As they drew nearer, one of the light-and-shadow beings turned toward them, its face a featureless mask of shifting shades. Despite its lack of distinct features, the being radiated a sense of calm and peacefulness.

"Welcome to the Realm of Duality," the figure said, its voice a soft blend of harmony and echo. "You have entered a world where light and shadow must coexist in perfect balance. Without one, the other cannot exist."

"Why are you dancing?" Rafi asked, his wings fluttering as he observed the figures moving in unison.

"We dance because it is the only way to maintain the balance," the figure explained. "Here, light and shadow must always be in motion, always in harmony. If the dance stops, the balance will be broken, and chaos will reign."

The group exchanged glances, understanding that they had entered a realm where the very fabric of the world depended on the delicate equilibrium between opposites. They had seen contrasts before—night and day, happiness and sorrow—but this place seemed to embody the idea that these opposing forces were not enemies, but partners.

"Is that why we're here?" Ellie asked. "To learn how to keep the balance?"

The figure nodded. "In every world, in every being, there are shadows and light. To truly understand yourselves, you must learn to dance with both."

The group stood in silence for a moment, contemplating the figure's words. They each carried their own shadows—their doubts, fears, and insecurities—and their own light—their hopes, dreams, and strengths. But until now, they had never considered that these two aspects of themselves were not separate, but intertwined.

"I think I understand," Lila said quietly. "We can't reject the darker parts of ourselves, or we lose the balance. We have to embrace both the light and the shadow."

"Exactly," the figure replied. "Now, it is time for you to join the dance."

Before anyone could respond, the ground beneath them shifted, and the group found themselves standing in the center of a large, circular platform. Around them, the light-and-shadow figures continued their graceful movements, their steps precise and fluid, always maintaining a perfect equilibrium.

"You must each find your own partner," the figure instructed. "One of you must dance with your light, and the other with your shadow."

The group hesitated. The idea of dancing with something as intangible as light and shadow felt strange, even daunting. But they knew that this was a part of their journey, a lesson they needed to learn.

Rafi was the first to step forward. His wings spread wide as he looked up at the sky, which was a swirling blend of bright sunlight and deep twilight. "I'll dance with the light," he said, a smile playing on his lips. "It's always been where I feel most at home."

The moment he spoke, a beam of light descended from above, wrapping around him like a warm embrace. The light shimmered and shifted, taking the shape of a partner made entirely of glowing radiance. Together, Rafi and the being of light began to move, their steps in perfect sync as they glided across the platform.

Lila was next. She took a deep breath and stepped toward one of the shadowy figures, her green hair glowing faintly in the dim light. "I'll dance with the shadow," she said. "I've always felt a connection to the darker, quieter parts of the world."

As soon as she spoke, a shadow detached itself from the ground and formed into a partner beside her. The two began to dance, their movements slower and more deliberate than Rafi's, but no less graceful.

One by one, the rest of the group joined the dance. Ellie found herself dancing with a being made of soft twilight, somewhere between light and shadow. Coralia's partner was a swirling mist of darkness, while Zephyr moved with a figure that shifted between storm clouds and beams of sunlight.

As they danced, the group began to feel the balance within themselves. They realized that the light and shadow were not opposing forces to be fought, but parts of a whole. The dance was not about domination or control, but about harmony—about allowing both aspects of themselves to move in unison.

As the dance continued, the platform beneath them glowed brighter, as though the world itself was responding to their newfound understanding. The air hummed with energy, and the light-and-shadow figures around them seemed to glow with approval.

When the dance finally ended, the group stood together, their hearts filled with a sense of peace and balance they had never felt before.

"You have learned the lesson of the Dance of Shadows and Light," the figure said. "Remember this: there is no light without shadow, and no shadow without light. To truly understand yourselves and the world around you, you must embrace both."

Lessons Learned

1. **Balance is essential** – light and shadow must coexist in harmony.
2. **Embrace all parts of yourself** – both light and shadow are necessary to understand the whole self.
3. **Opposites are not enemies** – light and shadow are partners, not adversaries.
4. **Harmony requires movement** – balance is not static; it must be actively maintained.
5. **Self-acceptance comes from within** – understanding both

strengths and weaknesses leads to peace.

6. **Shadows have value** – the darker aspects of ourselves are just as important as the light.
7. **Light cannot exist alone** – even the brightest light needs shadow to define it.
8. **Growth comes from duality** – embracing both light and dark allows for deeper self-understanding.
9. **Contrasts define beauty** – the dance of light and shadow creates something more beautiful than either alone.
10. **Strength comes from balance** – true strength is found in the harmony of opposites.

Chapter 7: Voices of the Earth

The forest stretched out before the group like a vast, green ocean, the canopy of trees so thick that it blocked out most of the sunlight. The air was cool and fresh, filled with the scent of damp earth and the distant sound of rustling leaves. As they ventured deeper into the forest, a sense of calm and stillness washed over them, as if the very ground beneath their feet was alive with quiet energy.

"This place feels... alive," Ellie whispered, her voice barely audible in the stillness.

"It is," Lila replied, her green hair shimmering in the dappled light. "The earth speaks here. If you listen closely, you can hear its voice."

The group paused, listening intently to the forest around them. At first, all they could hear was the sound of the wind rustling through the leaves and the distant call of birds. But as they stood in silence, they began to notice something else—a soft, almost imperceptible hum that seemed to come from the ground itself.

"Do you hear that?" Rafi asked, his wings twitching slightly.

Lila nodded. "It's the voice of the earth. Every tree, every plant, every stone has its own song. They're all connected, like a giant web of life."

Zephyr, ever the skeptic, frowned. "I don't hear anything," he said, his deep voice breaking the stillness.

"That's because you're not listening with your heart," Lila replied. "The earth doesn't speak in words. It speaks in feelings, in vibrations. You have to be open to it."

The group continued their journey through the forest, each of them trying to tune into the subtle vibrations of the earth beneath their feet. As they walked, they began to notice how the trees seemed to lean toward them, their branches swaying gently as if acknowledging their presence. The leaves whispered secrets, and the flowers seemed to glow faintly in the soft light.

After some time, they came across a massive, ancient tree in the heart of the forest. Its trunk was wider than any they had ever seen, and its roots spread out across the ground like giant serpents, intertwining with the earth itself. The tree seemed to pulse with a quiet, steady energy, and the air around it was thick with the feeling of ancient wisdom.

"This must be the heart of the forest," Lila said, her voice filled with reverence.

As they approached the tree, they noticed something strange. The roots seemed to form a path, leading deep into the forest. Without a word, they followed the path, their footsteps light and careful. The deeper they went, the more the forest seemed to come alive around them. The trees whispered louder, and the ground beneath their feet pulsed with a steady rhythm, like the heartbeat of the earth itself.

Finally, they reached a clearing where a circle of stones stood in the center. Each stone was covered in moss and vines, and they seemed to hum with energy. In the center of the circle was a small, glowing flower, its petals shimmering with a soft, golden light.

"This is it," Lila whispered. "The voice of the earth."

The group stood in silence, feeling the energy of the place wash over them. The air was thick with the feeling of connection, as if the entire forest was speaking to them in a language that transcended words.

"The earth speaks to those who listen," a voice said, and the group turned to see an old woman standing at the edge of the clearing. Her hair was gray and wild, and her eyes sparkled with the wisdom of ages.

"Who are you?" Coralia asked, her voice filled with curiosity.

"I am the Guardian of the Forest," the woman replied. "I protect this place and keep the balance between the earth and those who walk upon it."

"Why did you bring us here?" Ellie asked.

The Guardian smiled. "You were not brought here. You were guided. The earth itself has called you to this place to teach you its secrets. To truly understand the world around you, you must learn to listen to the voices of the earth. Every tree, every flower, every stone has a story to tell."

The group stood in awe, realizing that they had been given a rare and precious gift—the ability to communicate with the very fabric of nature.

"How do we learn to listen?" Rafi asked.

The Guardian stepped forward and placed her hand on the trunk of the ancient tree. "You must be still," she said. "You must quiet your mind and open your heart. The earth's voice is subtle, but it is always there. It speaks in the rustle of leaves, in the trickle of water, in the shifting of stones. You must learn to feel its presence and understand its message."

One by one, the group placed their hands on the ancient tree, feeling the steady pulse of energy beneath their fingertips. As they stood there, they began to feel a deep sense of connection—to the earth, to the trees, to each other. The ground beneath them seemed to hum with life, and they could feel the vibrations of the forest flowing through their bodies.

In that moment, they understood. The earth was not just a place to walk upon or a resource to use. It was alive, a living, breathing entity with its own thoughts, feelings, and stories. And they were a part of it.

As they stood in the clearing, the earth whispered its secrets to them. It spoke of ancient times, of forgotten civilizations, of the balance between life and death, growth and decay. It reminded them that everything was connected, that every action had a consequence, and that the health of the earth was tied to the health of all living things.

Lessons Learned

1. **The earth is alive** – the forest and everything in it have their own voices and stories.
2. **Connection to nature** – humans and nature are deeply intertwined, and understanding this connection is essential.
3. **Stillness leads to understanding** – by quieting their minds, the group was able to hear the voices of the earth.
4. **Balance is key** – the earth's health is tied to the balance of all living things.
5. **Respect for nature** – the group learned to respect the forest and the life it contained.
6. **Everything is connected** – the earth reminded them that all life is interconnected.
7. **Ancient wisdom** – the earth holds the secrets of the past, and it can teach those who listen.
8. **Nature is not a resource** – the earth is not something to be used, but something to be honored and protected.
9. **Every action has a consequence** – the group realized that their actions affect the world around them in profound ways.
10. **Gratitude for the earth** – they left the forest with a deep sense of gratitude for the lessons they had learned.

Chapter 8: The Taste of the World

After their time in the forest, the group found themselves in a new land, one that was filled with the most delicious aromas they had ever encountered. The air was thick with the scent of spices, fresh bread, roasting meats, and sweet pastries. Their mouths watered as they stepped into a bustling marketplace, where people from all corners of the world were gathered, sharing food and stories.

"I've never smelled anything so good in my life," Rafi said, his wings fluttering in excitement.

"It's like the whole world is here," Coralia added, her eyes wide as she took in the vibrant colors of the marketplace stalls.

The marketplace was a feast for the senses. Brightly colored fabrics draped over the stalls, and vendors called out to passersby, offering samples of their dishes. There were foods from every imaginable culture—spicy curries, tangy pickles, rich stews, sweet cakes, and savory pies. Each stall seemed to represent a different part of the world, and the people gathered there were as diverse as the food itself.

As they wandered through the marketplace, the group was greeted by a friendly man with a wide smile. He was dressed in vibrant robes, and his stall was filled with steaming pots of food.

"Welcome, travelers!" he called out. "You've arrived just in time for the Feast of the World. Please, come and join us!"

"The Feast of the World?" Lila asked, intrigued.

"Yes!" the man replied. "Once a year, people from all over gather here to share their food, their stories, and their cultures. It's a celebration of diversity, of the many flavors that make our world so rich and beautiful. And today, you are our honored guests."

The group smiled, excited by the idea of sharing in this celebration. They were invited to sit at a long table that stretched through the center of the marketplace, where people from all walks of life were seated, passing dishes back and forth, laughing, and sharing stories.

As they took their seats, the man brought them a plate filled with a variety of foods from different stalls. "Eat, enjoy!" he said with a grin. "And if you have a dish from your own culture, we'd love to taste it."

The group exchanged glances, realizing that they had an opportunity to not only enjoy the food but to share a piece of their own cultures with the people around them.

Ellie was the first to speak. "In my village by the sea, we make a dish called seaflower stew," she said, her eyes lighting up as she described the meal. "It's made with fresh fish, seaweed, and flowers that grow along the shore. It's a dish we make to celebrate the ocean and the life it gives us."

The man's eyes widened with interest. "That sounds wonderful! Would you be willing to make it for us?"

Ellie nodded eagerly, and the man led her to a stall where she could prepare the dish. As she worked, the group shared stories of their own food traditions.

"In my village," Lila said, "we make a dish called Forest Harvest Pie. It's filled with mushrooms, herbs, and berries that we gather from the forest. It's a dish that celebrates the changing seasons and the gifts of the earth."

Zephyr, who had been quietly observing the marketplace, finally spoke up. "In my kingdom, we eat a dish called Stormbread. It's a dense, hearty bread made during the winter storms. It's baked in the heat of the lightning and is said to give strength and courage to those who eat it."

Rafi, ever the adventurer, shared his own story. "In my village, we make Skyfruit Jam. It's made from a fruit that grows only on the highest cliffs, and it's so sweet that it tastes like the sky itself. We eat it when we celebrate a successful flight."

Coralia smiled as she added, "In the underwater cities, we have a dish called Coral Crisp. It's made from crunchy sea plants and served with a sauce made from pearls. It's our way of honoring the beauty and strength of the ocean."

As they shared their stories, the group realized that each dish was more than just food. It was a reflection of their culture, their history, and their connection to the world around them. And as they tasted the dishes from other cultures, they began to understand that food was a universal language, a way to connect with others and share in the richness of life.

When Ellie's seaflower stew was ready, she brought it to the table, and the people around her eagerly tried it. The man who had welcomed them smiled as he tasted the stew. "Delicious!" he exclaimed. "You've brought the ocean to our table."

One by one, the group shared their dishes with the people of the marketplace, and in return, they were invited to try foods from every corner of the world. They tasted spicy dishes from distant lands, sweet treats from desert oases, and rich stews from mountain villages. Each dish was a new adventure, a new story waiting to be told.

By the end of the feast, the group was full not only from the food but from the sense of connection they had felt with the people around them. They had shared their cultures, their traditions, and their stories, and in doing so, they had learned that the world was a vast and beautiful place, filled with endless flavors and experiences.

As they said their goodbyes to the people of the marketplace, the man who had welcomed them gave each of them a small, intricately carved wooden spoon. "A gift," he said with a wink. "To remind you of the Feast of the World and the many flavors that make life so rich."

Lessons Learned

1. **Food is a universal language** – it connects people from different cultures and brings them together.
2. **Every dish tells a story** – the food they shared was a reflection of their history, culture, and values.

3. **Diversity enriches life** – the variety of flavors and traditions made the Feast of the World a beautiful celebration of diversity.
4. **Cultural exchange is powerful** – by sharing their food, they learned about the world and each other.
5. **Celebration through food** – food is more than sustenance; it's a way to celebrate life and the world around us.
6. **Honoring traditions** – each dish they shared was a way of honoring their culture and their connection to their homeland.
7. **Learning through experience** – tasting new foods helped them understand other cultures in a meaningful way.
8. **Gratitude for diversity** – the group left the feast with a deep appreciation for the richness that diversity brings to the world.
9. **Unity in difference** – despite their different backgrounds, they all shared in the joy of the feast.
10. **Memories are shared** – the wooden spoons were a reminder that the experiences they shared would stay with them forever.

Chapter 9: A Journey Through Time

The sky above them began to swirl with strange colors as the group entered a realm that felt both familiar and alien at the same time. The air around them was thick with the feeling of time itself, as though they were standing at the intersection of past, present, and future all at once.

"What is this place?" Rafi asked, his wings fluttering nervously as he looked around.

"I don't know," Ellie replied, her voice quiet with awe. "But it feels like time is... different here."

As they walked deeper into the realm, they noticed that the landscape around them seemed to shift and change with every step they took. One moment, they were standing in a lush green field, and the next, they were walking through the ruins of an ancient city. Time moved fluidly in this place, as though the past and present were constantly intertwining.

Suddenly, they came across a massive stone archway, covered in vines and moss. At the top of the archway, a symbol was carved into the stone—a circle divided in half, with one side representing the sun and the other representing the moon.

"This must be the gateway," Lila said, her voice filled with wonder.

"The gateway to what?" Coralia asked, her tail flicking nervously.

Before anyone could answer, the ground beneath them began to glow with a soft, golden light. The air around them shimmered, and in an instant, they were no longer standing in the realm of swirling time. Instead, they found themselves in a familiar setting—each of them standing in a place from their past.

Ellie was standing on the shore of her seaside village, the salty breeze blowing through her hair as she watched the waves crash against the rocks. It was a place she knew well, a place where she had spent countless hours staring out at the horizon, wondering what lay beyond.

Rafi found himself standing at the edge of a cliff, the wind whipping through his hair as he prepared to take flight. This was the place where he had first learned to fly, where he had spent hours practicing his skills and dreaming of soaring higher and farther than anyone had ever gone before.

Lila was in the heart of the forest, surrounded by towering trees and the sounds of birds and animals. This was her sanctuary, the place where she had always felt most at home, most connected to the world around her.

Coralia was deep beneath the ocean, swimming through the shimmering coral reefs that surrounded her underwater city. It was a place of beauty and wonder, a place where she had always felt safe and free.

Zephyr found himself standing in the middle of a storm, the wind and rain lashing against his body as lightning crackled overhead. This was the place where he had first learned the true power of the storm, where he had discovered the strength that lay within him.

For a moment, each of them stood frozen in their memories, overwhelmed by the flood of emotions that came with being back in these familiar places. But as they looked around, they began to notice something strange. Time was not moving as it should. The waves of the ocean were frozen in place, the birds in the trees were still, and the storm around Zephyr hung in the air, suspended in time.

"What's happening?" Ellie asked, her voice filled with confusion.

"It's like time has stopped," Rafi replied, his eyes wide as he looked around.

Before they could fully process what was happening, a soft voice spoke, seemingly from everywhere and nowhere at once. "You are standing in the realm of time, where the past, present, and future are intertwined. Here, you will walk through your memories, and you will see how your experiences have shaped who you are."

The group exchanged nervous glances, unsure of what to expect.

As they continued to explore their surroundings, they began to notice that their memories were not exactly as they remembered. There were subtle differences, moments they had forgotten or overlooked, things they had never fully understood.

For Ellie, it was the memory of her father, standing beside her on the shore as they watched the waves together. She had always remembered him as quiet and distant, but now, as she stood in this moment, she realized that he had been watching the horizon just as she had, dreaming of the world beyond the sea.

For Rafi, it was the memory of his first flight. He had always remembered it as a moment of triumph, but now, as he stood on the edge of the cliff, he noticed the fear that had been in his heart, the uncertainty that had clouded his mind before he had taken that first leap.

Lila's memory was of a time when she had felt lost, disconnected from the world around her. She had wandered through the forest, feeling as though she didn't belong anywhere. But now, as she stood in that same place, she realized that the forest had been speaking to her all along, trying to guide her back to herself.

Coralia's memory was of the first time she had ventured into the deeper parts of the ocean, far beyond the safety of the reefs. She had always remembered it as an adventure, but now, as she swam through the memory, she felt the fear that had gripped her heart, the uncertainty of the unknown.

For Zephyr, the memory was of a storm that had nearly overwhelmed him. He had always seen it as a test of his strength, a battle he had fought and won. But now, as he stood in the heart of the storm, he realized that it had been a moment of vulnerability, a time when he had come close to losing control.

As they walked through their memories, the group began to understand that their pasts were not as simple as they had always believed. There were layers to their experiences, moments of fear and uncertainty, but also moments of strength and resilience.

"The past shapes who we are," the voice said. "But it does not define us. It is only through understanding our experiences, both the light and the dark, that we can truly grow."

Lessons Learned

1. **The past shapes us** – their experiences, both good and bad, have made them who they are.
2. **Understanding brings growth** – by revisiting their memories, they gained a deeper understanding of themselves.
3. **Fear is a part of the journey** – moments of fear and uncertainty are just as important as moments of triumph.
4. **Resilience comes from struggle** – the challenges they faced in the past gave them the strength they needed for the future.
5. **The past is not fixed** – their memories were not exactly as they remembered, showing that the past is always evolving.
6. **Both light and dark matter** – understanding both the positive and negative aspects of their experiences was key to their growth.
7. **We are not defined by our past** – while the past shapes us, it does not define who we are.
8. **Growth comes from reflection** – by reflecting on their pasts, they were able to see how far they had come.
9. **Vulnerability is strength** – moments of vulnerability were a source of strength, not weakness.
10. **The journey continues** – the lessons of the past will guide them, but the journey of growth is ongoing.

Chapter 10: The Language of Touch

The world they entered next was unlike any they had encountered before. As they stepped through the portal, the group found themselves in a land that was completely silent. The wind did not rustle the leaves, the water did not babble in the streams, and even their own voices seemed to be swallowed by the stillness.

Ellie tried to speak, but no sound came from her lips. She looked at the others, her eyes wide with confusion.

"I can't hear anything," Rafi mouthed, his expression mirroring Ellie's confusion. He flapped his wings, but even the familiar sound of the wind rushing through his feathers was absent.

The group exchanged worried glances, unsure of what to do. They had always relied on their voices to communicate, to share their thoughts and ideas. Without sound, they felt disconnected, lost.

Lila, ever attuned to the natural world, closed her eyes and placed her hand on the ground. She felt a faint vibration beneath her fingertips, a subtle rhythm that seemed to pulse through the earth.

"It's not completely silent," she mouthed, her fingers brushing the grass. "There's something here. We just have to feel it."

The group followed Lila's lead, placing their hands on the ground, on trees, on stones. As they did, they began to feel the faint vibrations, the quiet hum of life that pulsed through the land. It was a language, but one that could not be heard. It had to be felt.

Zephyr, always the most tactile of the group, spread his wings wide and let the breeze brush against them. He felt the subtle shifts in the air, the gentle pressure of the wind against his feathers. It was a conversation, but one spoken in touch rather than sound.

As they explored the silent world, they began to understand that communication here was not about words or voices. It was about touch, about the subtle ways in which the world spoke through vibrations, pressure, and movement. They learned to communicate with each other through gestures, through the way they moved their bodies and the way they touched the world around them.

Ellie, who had always relied on her voice to express herself, found herself struggling at first. She was used to speaking her thoughts out loud, to using words to connect with others. But as the group continued their journey through the silent land, she began to notice the way her body moved in response to the world around her. She realized that she could communicate without words, through the way she touched the earth, the way she moved her hands and feet.

Coralia, who had always been more reserved, found comfort in the silence. She had never been one for speaking much, preferring to let her actions speak for her. In this world, she felt at home, using touch and movement to express herself in ways that words never could.

Rafi, ever the adventurer, found joy in the challenge of learning a new language. He experimented with different ways of moving, of touching the world around him, and found that he could communicate just as effectively without words as he could with them.

Zephyr, with his powerful wings and strong body, found that the world responded to his touch in ways he had never noticed before. The wind shifted around him, the earth seemed to hum beneath his feet, and even the trees swayed gently in response to his presence.

As they continued their journey, the group learned to rely on each other in new ways. Without words, they had to trust their instincts, to read each other's movements and gestures. They became more attuned to the subtle ways in which their bodies communicated, and they found that they could understand each other without ever speaking a word.

In this silent world, they learned the importance of touch, of connection that went beyond words. They realized that communication was not just about speaking, but about feeling, about being present in the moment and truly connecting with the world and with each other.

At the end of their journey through the silent land, the group came across a massive stone wall, covered in intricate carvings. The carvings depicted scenes of people and animals, all engaged in various forms of communication—gestures, touches, movements. It was a reminder that language was more than just words. It was a way of connecting, of understanding, of being understood.

"The language of touch is the language of connection," the wall seemed to say. "It is a language that transcends words, a language that speaks to the heart and the soul."

The group stood in silence, feeling the truth of those words deep within themselves. They had learned a new way of communicating, a way that went beyond sound and speech. They had learned to listen with their hearts, to feel with their souls.

Lessons Learned

1. **Communication is more than words** – they learned to communicate through touch and movement, rather than speech.
2. **Touch connects us** – the silent land taught them that touch is a powerful form of connection.
3. **Listening with the heart** – they learned to listen not with their ears, but with their hearts and bodies.
4. **Presence is key** – being present in the moment allowed them to truly connect with the world around them.
5. **Body language speaks volumes** – they learned to read each other's movements and gestures, understanding without words.
6. **Trust in intuition** – without words, they had to trust their instincts and intuition to communicate.
7. **Silence can be powerful** – the silence of the land was not empty; it was filled with meaning and connection.
8. **Different forms of communication** – they learned that

there are many ways to communicate, beyond just speaking.

9. **Connection through feeling** – they realized that feeling and touch could create deep connections.
10. **The power of non-verbal communication** – they discovered the importance of non-verbal communication in building trust and understanding.

Chapter 11: Through the Eyes of Another

The morning was as ordinary as any could be, with the familiar rustling of trees and the soft songs of birds filling the air. The group had grown comfortable with the unexpected on their journey, yet nothing could have prepared them for what was about to unfold. As they set off from their campsite, they walked through a lush valley where the grass was taller than Rafi's knees and the air hummed with the life of a world blooming into full vibrancy.

"This place feels different," Lila observed, brushing her hand through the tall blades of grass. "There's something... off. But I can't quite put my finger on it."

Coralia, who had been floating in a nearby stream, nodded thoughtfully. "It's as if the world itself is watching us."

Rafi flexed his wings, preparing to take flight when a shimmering light appeared before them. It wasn't the first magical anomaly they had encountered, but this light was different—ethereal and delicate, as if the air itself had turned to glass and refracted the sun into a million shades of color. Without a word, they stepped toward it.

Suddenly, everything shifted.

The world tilted, spun, and rearranged itself in a way that defied logic. One moment, Ellie was looking at Rafi preparing for flight, and the next, she was in the air, her wings beating against the wind. Except, they weren't her wings at all. She looked down at herself—no, at Rafi's body—and a wave of confusion swept over her. She wasn't Ellie anymore. She was Rafi.

"What's happening?" Ellie's voice echoed from Rafi's body, but it wasn't her voice—it was his.

At the same time, the others realized they too had switched bodies. Lila found herself in Zephyr's form, towering over the group, her paws heavy against the earth, while Coralia, usually graceful in her aquatic form, now stood as Ellie, feeling the unfamiliar sensation of legs instead of fins. Zephyr, for his part, flapped Rafi's wings clumsily, unaccustomed to the sensation of weightlessness.

"This is... incredible," Rafi, now in Lila's body, whispered, his voice full of awe. He stretched out Lila's hands and watched as the vines around them responded to his touch. "I can feel everything the forest feels."

The group stood in stunned silence for a moment before bursting into conversation, each of them marveling at their new forms, laughing awkwardly as they tried to adjust. Zephyr attempted to leap into the air with Rafi's wings but found himself spinning and tumbling clumsily to the ground. Coralia tried to walk as Ellie but stumbled, unfamiliar with moving on land.

It was strange, disorienting, and exhilarating all at once. But soon, they began to realize the deeper meaning of what had happened. They weren't just playing around in each other's bodies; they were experiencing the world from a completely different perspective. Each challenge they faced, each new sensation, was teaching them something vital about their companions.

Ellie, now in Rafi's body, was the first to experience the weight of his wings. What had always seemed like an effortless skill—soaring through the skies—was suddenly a difficult and exhausting task. She tried to lift off the ground, feeling the strain of muscles she had never used before. It wasn't just physical effort; it was a mental battle to coordinate the delicate balance required for flight.

Rafi, meanwhile, was feeling the deep connection Lila had to the forest. He could hear the whispers of the trees, feel the hum of life in the soil beneath his feet. It was overwhelming at first, like trying to listen to a hundred conversations at once, but as he focused, he began to understand the quiet wisdom of the natural world. It was a connection he had never felt before, a reminder that there was power in the stillness of the earth as much as in the freedom of the skies.

Zephyr, in Rafi's much smaller body, was grappling with vulnerability. He had always been the strongest, the one who could protect the group with his physical presence. But now, in a smaller, more delicate form, he felt exposed. He realized how much courage it took for Rafi to venture into the unknown, relying on his agility and speed rather than sheer strength.

Coralia, as Ellie, experienced the pull of the ocean from a distance. She could no longer dive into the water, and the lack of connection to her familiar world made her feel adrift. But in Ellie's body, she began to understand the quiet determination Ellie carried. Though she was often on land, Ellie always had the ocean in her heart, its rhythms influencing her every decision, grounding her in a way Coralia hadn't fully appreciated before.

Lila, now towering in Zephyr's mighty form, felt the burden of leadership. She had always admired Zephyr's strength, but now she understood the weight of responsibility he carried. Being strong wasn't just about physical power; it was about protecting those around you, being a pillar of support in times of danger. She realized how much Zephyr had to sacrifice his own needs to care for the group, and how difficult it must be to balance strength with gentleness.

As the day went on, the group continued to explore their new forms, each of them learning to navigate the challenges and joys of their friends' lives. By the time the sun began to set, they had a newfound respect for one another—a deep understanding that went beyond words.

When the shimmering light reappeared at dusk, they knew their time in each other's bodies was coming to an end. With a flash, they were back in their original forms, the familiar weight of their own bodies grounding them once more. But they were changed. They had walked in each other's shoes, felt the world through each other's senses, and now, they saw one another with new eyes.

Lessons Learned

1. **Empathy comes from experience** – by living in each other's bodies, they gained a deep understanding of the challenges their friends faced.
2. **Perspective shapes understanding** – seeing the world from a different perspective helped them appreciate their friends' strengths and struggles.
3. **We all carry hidden burdens** – they realized that everyone has challenges, even if they aren't always visible.
4. **Strength comes in many forms** – physical strength, emotional resilience, and connection to nature are all different types of strength.
5. **Diversity is a source of strength** – their differences made the group stronger, as each person brought something unique to the table.
6. **Vulnerability is part of courage** – they learned that being vulnerable doesn't mean being weak; it means having the courage to face challenges.
7. **Appreciating others' gifts** – by walking in each other's shoes, they gained a new appreciation for the gifts their friends possessed.
8. **Balance between independence and interdependence** – they saw how their individual strengths and weaknesses complemented one another.
9. **Understanding leads to unity** – their newfound empathy helped them feel more connected as a group.
10. **We are all more than we appear** – they realized that everyone has unseen depths, challenges, and strengths that are not always visible on the surface.

Chapter 12: The Heart of the Sea

The wind had begun to shift, carrying with it the unmistakable scent of salt and the distant roar of waves crashing against rocks. Coralia was the first to notice, her senses finely tuned to the call of the ocean. She raised her head and smiled as they neared the coastline. The sound of the sea filled her heart with a sense of homecoming, and she beckoned the others toward the water's edge.

"This is where I belong," Coralia said, her voice soft but filled with pride. "The ocean is more than just my home. It's a world full of life, beauty, and mystery."

The group followed her as the land gave way to golden sands, and the shimmering blue expanse of the sea spread out before them. The water sparkled beneath the midday sun, and the waves seemed to beckon them forward, inviting them to explore the mysteries beneath the surface.

"I've never been under the sea before," Ellie admitted, her eyes wide with curiosity as she watched the waves lap against the shore.

"You're in for a treat," Coralia said with a grin. "The ocean is full of wonders you can't even imagine."

With a quick dive, Coralia disappeared beneath the surface, her form blending seamlessly with the water. One by one, the others followed her lead. As they plunged into the cool depths, a magical transformation occurred. Their bodies adapted to the underwater world—Ellie's legs became a sleek tail, and Rafi's wings transformed into graceful fins. Even Zephyr, large as he was, found himself moving through the water with surprising ease.

The world beneath the waves was unlike anything they had ever seen. It was a vibrant, living tapestry of colors, sounds, and textures. Schools of fish darted around them in shimmering clouds of silver, while coral reefs bloomed in every shade imaginable. The light filtered through the water, casting a gentle glow on everything it touched, and the currents swirled in a rhythm that felt both soothing and powerful.

"This is incredible," Lila said, her voice a soft hum through the water. "It's like an entirely different world."

"It is," Coralia agreed, swimming beside her. "Everything down here is connected. The ocean is a vast ecosystem, and every creature, no matter how small, plays a part in keeping it alive."

As they swam deeper, the group encountered a wide variety of marine creatures, each more fascinating than the last. They passed a colony of sea turtles, gliding gracefully through the water, and watched as a pod of dolphins played in the currents above them. A school of jellyfish floated by, their translucent bodies pulsing with a gentle, otherworldly light.

But as they ventured farther into the heart of the sea, the atmosphere began to change. The water grew darker, and the currents stronger. The vibrant colors of the coral reef gave way to a barren, lifeless landscape of rocky cliffs and deep chasms.

"What happened here?" Zephyr asked, his voice tinged with concern.

Coralia's expression grew somber. "This is the result of imbalance," she explained. "Something has disrupted the natural order of the ocean. Without balance, entire ecosystems can collapse."

As they swam through the desolate waters, the group encountered creatures struggling to survive in the changing environment. Fish swam aimlessly, unable to find food, and the coral that once provided shelter for countless species had turned white and brittle, bleached by the stress of the changing conditions.

"We have to do something," Ellie said, her heart aching for the creatures around her.

"We will," Coralia replied, determination in her voice. "But first, we need to understand what caused this imbalance."

They continued their journey through the heart of the sea, searching for clues to the cause of the devastation. As they swam deeper, they came across a massive whirlpool, its dark waters churning with an unnatural energy.

"This is it," Coralia said, her eyes narrowing. "This whirlpool is disrupting the natural flow of the ocean's currents. It's pulling everything out of balance."

"How do we stop it?" Rafi asked, his fins twitching nervously.

"We need to redirect the energy," Coralia explained. "The ocean is a powerful force, but it can be guided. If we work together, we can restore the balance."

The group nodded in agreement, each of them ready to do whatever it took to help the ocean heal. They swam toward the whirlpool, feeling the pull of its chaotic energy as they approached. It was a daunting task, but they knew they had to try.

Coralia took the lead, using her connection to the sea to guide the flow of energy. Ellie, Rafi, Lila, and Zephyr followed her movements, adding their own strength to the effort. Together, they created a new current, one that pushed against the whirlpool's destructive force.

Slowly but surely, the whirlpool began to weaken. The water's chaotic churning subsided, and the ocean's natural rhythms started to return. The currents flowed more gently, and the once-dark waters grew lighter as life returned to the surrounding area.

When the whirlpool finally dissolved, the group watched in awe as the ocean around them began to heal. The coral reefs, once bleached and lifeless, started to regain their color, and the fish returned to their homes. The balance of the ocean had been restored.

Lessons Learned

1. **Balance is essential for life** – the ocean's ecosystems rely on balance to survive, and when that balance is disrupted, the consequences are devastating.

2. **Everything is connected** – every creature in the ocean, no matter how small, plays a role in maintaining the health of the ecosystem.
3. **Respect for nature** – the ocean is a powerful force, but it is also fragile and in need of protection.
4. **Collaboration leads to healing** – by working together, the group was able to restore balance to the ocean.
5. **Adaptation is key to survival** – the marine creatures had to adapt to the changing environment, just as the group had to adapt to the underwater world.
6. **Nature's power can be guided** – while the ocean's currents are strong, they can be redirected and guided toward positive change.
7. **Vigilance is necessary** – balance is not something that can be achieved once and then forgotten; it requires constant attention and care.
8. **Empathy for all life** – the group's hearts ached for the creatures affected by the imbalance, teaching them the importance of empathy for all living beings.
9. **Environmental stewardship** – they learned that it was their responsibility to protect and care for the natural world.
10. **The beauty of diversity** – the ocean is home to an incredible diversity of life, and each species contributes to the overall health of the ecosystem.

Chapter 13: The Power of Stories

The evening was calm as the group gathered around a small fire on the edge of the forest. The night sky above them was a deep indigo, and the stars sparkled like diamonds scattered across velvet. After the intense journey through the heart of the sea, the quiet serenity of the night felt like a welcome relief. As they settled down, the flickering flames cast long shadows on the ground, and the group found themselves drawn into a quiet, reflective mood.

"I've been thinking," Ellie said softly, breaking the silence. "About how everything we've been through has shaped us. Every place we've visited, every challenge we've faced... it's all part of our story."

The others nodded in agreement. They had been on an incredible journey, one that had changed them in ways they hadn't even fully realized yet. But it wasn't just the journey itself that had shaped them—it was the stories they had carried with them from the very beginning.

"Stories are powerful," Lila mused, her green hair glowing faintly in the firelight. "They connect us to the past, to each other, and to the world around us."

Rafi, always the adventurer, smiled. "I love stories. My people tell them all the time—stories about the sky, about flying, about the stars. They remind us of who we are and where we come from."

Zephyr, his large form casting a shadow over the group, nodded thoughtfully. "In my kingdom, stories are told to teach lessons. Every tale has a purpose, a meaning that helps guide us through life."

Coralia, sitting quietly beside the fire, finally spoke. "In the ocean, we tell stories through songs. The currents carry our voices, and the rhythm of the water weaves our stories together."

Ellie smiled, feeling a deep sense of connection to her friends. "Maybe tonight, we can share our stories with each other. We've all come from different places, and I think it would be wonderful to hear the stories that shaped us."

The group agreed, and one by one, they began to share the tales that had been passed down through their families, their cultures, and their experiences.

Ellie went first, her voice soft but clear as she recounted a story from her seaside village. "There's a story my mother used to tell me," she began, her eyes reflecting the firelight. "It's about a girl who lived by the sea, just like me. She was always curious, always looking out at the horizon, wondering what lay beyond the waves. One day, she met a dolphin who promised to take her to the farthest reaches of the ocean, where the sky touched the water and the stars danced on the waves. But the girl had to promise that she would always remember where she came from—that no matter how far she traveled, she would never forget her home."

The group listened intently as Ellie continued, the story weaving a beautiful tale of adventure, discovery, and the importance of remembering one's roots. When she finished, there was a moment of quiet reflection before Rafi spoke up.

"In my village," Rafi said, his voice full of excitement, "we tell a story about a great bird—the Sky King—who rules over the clouds. The Sky King is the fastest, strongest, most magnificent creature in the skies, and it's said that whoever can fly as high as the Sky King will be granted a wish. But the challenge isn't just about flying—it's about the courage to reach for something greater than yourself, to push past your limits."

Rafi's story was one of bravery and ambition, of striving for something beyond the ordinary. The group smiled as they listened, feeling inspired by the tale of reaching for the sky.

Lila's story was next, and as she spoke, her voice took on a soothing, melodic quality. "In the forest, we tell stories about the trees," she said. "There's one story in particular that's always stayed with me. It's about a young tree that grew in the shadow of a great oak. The young tree admired the oak, but it also felt small and insignificant in comparison. One day, a storm came, and the great oak was struck by lightning. The young tree was terrified, but when the storm passed, it realized that it had survived. And in the space where the oak had once stood, the young tree grew taller and stronger than ever before."

Lila's story was one of resilience and growth, of finding strength in the face of adversity. The group nodded in appreciation, understanding the deeper meaning behind the tale.

Zephyr's story came next, and his deep voice filled the night air as he spoke. "In my kingdom, we tell the story of the Thunderborn," he said. "The Thunderborn are warriors who are said to be born during the fiercest storms. They carry the strength of the storm within them, but they are also burdened by the weight of the thunder. It's said that the Thunderborn must learn to balance their strength with compassion, to use their power not for destruction, but for protection."

Zephyr's story was one of strength tempered by wisdom, of the responsibility that came with great power. The group listened closely, feeling the weight of the story's message.

Finally, it was Coralia's turn. Her voice was soft and rhythmic as she began her tale. "In the ocean, we tell the story of the Pearl of the Deep," she said. "It's said that deep beneath the waves, in the darkest part of the ocean, there lies a pearl of incredible beauty and power. But the pearl can only be found by those who are willing to dive into the unknown, to face the darkness and trust that they will find their way back to the light."

Coralia's story was one of courage and faith, of trusting in oneself and in the journey, even when the path was unclear. The group listened in silence, feeling the depth of the story resonate within them.

As the night grew darker and the fire began to burn lower, the group sat together in quiet contemplation. They had shared their stories, and in doing so, they had shared a part of themselves. The stories had connected them in a way that went beyond words, reminding them of the common threads that ran through their lives—love, courage, hope, and the search for meaning.

Lessons Learned

1. **Stories connect us** – sharing their stories helped the group understand each other on a deeper level.
2. **Identity is shaped by stories** – the tales they shared reflected their cultures, values, and experiences.
3. **Common themes of humanity** – despite their differences, their stories carried common themes of love, courage, and hope.
4. **Stories inspire growth** – each story contained a lesson or message that inspired the group to reflect on their own journey.
5. **Cultural richness** – the diversity of their stories showcased the richness of their different backgrounds and perspectives.
6. **The power of memory** – stories help keep memories and traditions alive, reminding them of where they come from.
7. **Courage and resilience** – many of the stories emphasized the importance of bravery and perseverance in the face of challenges.
8. **The importance of balance** – Zephyr's story about the Thunderborn highlighted the need to balance strength with compassion.
9. **Hope in the unknown** – Coralia's story reminded them of the importance of trusting in themselves, even when the path ahead is uncertain.
10. **The shared human experience** – though their stories were different, they all spoke to the shared experiences of life, growth, and connection.

Chapter 14: The Rainbow Bridge

The sky was a canvas of soft pastels as the group made their way through a peaceful valley. Above them, clouds drifted lazily, their edges kissed by the warm hues of the setting sun. The air was fresh and cool, and the path beneath their feet was lined with wildflowers in every color of the rainbow. It was a tranquil moment in their journey, but the group knew that another challenge lay ahead.

As they rounded a bend in the path, they came across a sight that took their breath away—a magnificent rainbow arched across the sky, its colors so vivid and bright that it seemed to shimmer with magic. But this was no ordinary rainbow. Instead of simply fading into the distance, the rainbow stretched down to the ground, forming a bridge that spanned a deep chasm in the earth.

"It's beautiful," Ellie whispered, her eyes wide with wonder.

"But it looks... fragile," Rafi said, eyeing the rainbow bridge warily. "How do we know it will hold us?"

Zephyr, always cautious, stepped forward and tested the first step of the bridge. The rainbow shimmered beneath his paw, but it held firm.

"It's stronger than it looks," Zephyr said, turning to the group. "But I can feel it—it requires more than just physical strength to cross."

Lila nodded, sensing the magic in the air. "This isn't just a bridge. It's a test. We'll need to be in harmony with ourselves and with each other to make it across."

The group exchanged glances, understanding that the rainbow bridge represented more than just a physical crossing. It was a symbol of unity, of self-acceptance, and of the strength that came from embracing their differences.

One by one, they stepped onto the bridge, each of them feeling the magic beneath their feet as they walked. The colors of the rainbow seemed to shift and change with each step, reflecting not only the light of the sun but the light within each of them.

As they crossed the bridge, they began to feel a change within themselves. The bridge wasn't just guiding them across the chasm—it was revealing their inner strengths and challenges, showing them the parts of themselves they had not fully embraced.

For Ellie, the bridge brought to the surface her quiet determination. She had always been the observer, the one who listened and watched from the sidelines. But as she walked across the rainbow, she realized that her quiet strength was just as powerful as Zephyr's physical strength or Rafi's courage. She didn't need to be loud or bold to make an impact—her strength came from within.

Rafi, always eager to take flight and soar to new heights, found himself confronted with his own impatience. The rainbow bridge required him to slow down, to walk steadily and carefully, rather than rushing ahead. It was a challenge for him to move at a different pace, but as he did, he realized that patience was a form of strength he had often overlooked.

Lila, who had always felt deeply connected to the earth and the natural world, felt the rainbow's colors illuminating her own inner conflict. She had always been focused on others—on the trees, the animals, the world around her—but the bridge reminded her that she needed to take care of herself as well. It was a lesson in balance, in recognizing that self-care was just as important as caring for the world.

Zephyr, who had always been the protector of the group, felt the weight of his responsibility as he walked across the rainbow. The colors of the bridge seemed to reflect his own sense of duty and strength, but they also revealed a softer side to him—a side that was compassionate and gentle. Zephyr realized that true strength wasn't just about being strong for others; it was also about allowing himself to be vulnerable.

Coralia, swimming gracefully through the air as if she were still in the ocean, felt the bridge's magic resonating with her sense of belonging. She had always been a creature of the sea, but as she crossed the rainbow, she felt a deep connection to the land as well. It was a reminder that she didn't have to choose between the ocean and the land—she could belong to both.

As they reached the midpoint of the bridge, a voice echoed around them, soft and melodic like the wind. "To cross the rainbow, you must embrace your true selves. Only by accepting your uniqueness can you unlock the strength to continue."

The group paused, reflecting on the voice's words. They had each faced challenges on their journey—challenges that had tested their courage, their resilience, and their connection to each other. But now, they were being asked to look inward, to embrace the parts of themselves that they had kept hidden or ignored.

Ellie took a deep breath and spoke first. "I've always been quiet," she said softly. "I've watched from the sidelines, thinking that I wasn't as strong or brave as the rest of you. But I'm realizing now that my quietness is part of my strength. I don't need to change who I am to be valuable."

Rafi nodded, his expression thoughtful. "I've always been in a hurry, always trying to move forward as fast as possible. But I'm learning that sometimes, slowing down and being patient is just as important as being bold."

Lila smiled, her eyes filled with understanding. "I've spent so much time taking care of the world around me that I've forgotten to take care of myself. But I'm starting to see that balance is the key to everything—balance between giving and receiving, between the world and myself."

Zephyr's deep voice rumbled with emotion. "I've always seen my strength as something I use to protect others. But I'm realizing that part of being strong is allowing myself to be vulnerable. I don't have to carry everything on my own."

Coralia's voice was soft but sure as she spoke. "I've always thought of myself as a creature of the ocean, but this journey has shown me that I can belong to more than one world. I can be both of the sea and of the land, and that doesn't make me any less."

As they each spoke their truths, the rainbow bridge shimmered brighter, its colors deepening and growing more vibrant. The group felt a surge of energy as they continued their journey across the bridge, their hearts lighter and their spirits stronger.

When they finally reached the other side, they looked back at the rainbow bridge, knowing that it had not only carried them across the chasm but had also carried them closer to themselves.

"We did it," Ellie said, a smile spreading across her face.

"We embraced who we are," Zephyr added, his voice filled with pride.

"And that's what gave us the strength to cross," Rafi finished, his wings stretching wide in triumph.

The group stood together, their bond stronger than ever. They had crossed the rainbow bridge, not just by relying on their physical strength, but by embracing their true selves and accepting the beauty of their differences.

Lessons Learned

1. **Self-acceptance is key** – embracing their true selves gave them the strength to cross the rainbow bridge.
2. **Quiet strength is powerful** – Ellie learned that her quiet determination was just as valuable as physical strength.
3. **Patience is a form of strength** – Rafi discovered that slowing down and being patient was a valuable lesson.
4. **Balance is essential** – Lila realized the importance of balancing self-care with caring for others.
5. **Strength comes from vulnerability** – Zephyr learned that allowing himself to be vulnerable was a sign of true strength.

6. **Belonging can be multifaceted** – Coralia found that she could belong to both the ocean and the land, without losing her sense of identity.
7. **Unity through individuality** – the group realized that their differences made them stronger together.
8. **True strength comes from within** – the bridge tested their inner strength, not just their physical abilities.
9. **Embracing uniqueness** – they learned that accepting their unique qualities was the key to unlocking their full potential.
10. **The journey of self-discovery** – crossing the rainbow bridge was a metaphor for their journey of self-discovery and growth.

Chapter 15: The Mirror of Many Faces

The group emerged from the forest into a clearing filled with towering mirrors, each one reflecting the world in strange and distorted ways. The mirrors were not like any they had ever seen before. They didn't just reflect the outside world; they seemed to show glimpses of the inner self, revealing parts of the soul that were usually hidden.

Lila was the first to step forward, her reflection rippling like water as she gazed into the mirror. But instead of seeing herself as she was, she saw many versions of herself—some small and timid, others tall and confident, and still others wise and serene. Each version of herself represented a different part of her identity, a different aspect of who she was.

"This is... strange," Lila whispered, her eyes wide as she looked at her many reflections. "It's like I'm seeing all the different parts of me at once."

Zephyr approached the nearest mirror, his massive frame casting a long shadow across the ground. When he looked into the mirror, he saw not just one reflection but many—some versions of himself were fierce and powerful, while others were gentle and calm. He realized that these mirrors were showing the many facets of his identity, the different sides of himself that he had never fully acknowledged.

As the others approached the mirrors, they too saw the multiple versions of themselves reflected back at them. Ellie saw herself as both the quiet observer and the determined leader. Rafi saw himself as the fearless adventurer but also as the cautious protector. Coralia saw herself as the creature of the sea, but also as someone who longed to explore the world beyond the ocean.

The group stood in silence, each of them captivated by the complexity of their reflections. The mirrors were showing them that they were not just one thing—they were made up of many different parts, each one equally important.

"This is who we are," Ellie said softly, her eyes filled with wonder. "We're not just one version of ourselves. We're many."

As they continued to explore the mirrors, they began to understand the importance of embracing the different facets of their identity. Each reflection was a part of them, and together, they formed a complete picture of who they were.

But as they moved deeper into the maze of mirrors, they began to encounter challenges. Some mirrors showed distorted versions of themselves—exaggerated weaknesses, fears, and insecurities. These reflections were harder to look at, but they knew they had to face them.

Lila found herself standing before a mirror that showed her as small and insignificant, her connection to the forest fading. It was a reflection of her deepest fear—that she would lose her sense of purpose, that her bond with nature would weaken. But as she looked closer, she realized that this fear was only one part of her, and that it didn't define her. She had the power to strengthen her connection to the world, to nurture it and help it grow.

Zephyr stood before a mirror that showed him as fierce and destructive, his strength used to cause harm rather than protect. It was a reflection of his fear that his power could be misused, that his strength could hurt those he loved. But as he faced this fear, he understood that true strength came from control and compassion. His power was a gift, and it was up to him to use it wisely.

Ellie's mirror showed her as a passive observer, watching the world pass by without ever taking action. It was a reflection of her fear that her quiet nature would prevent her from making a difference. But as she stared into the mirror, she realized that her quiet strength was her greatest asset. She didn't need to be loud or forceful to have an impact—she could lead with quiet determination and still make a difference.

Rafi's mirror showed him as reckless and impulsive, charging into danger without thinking. It was a reflection of his fear that his desire for adventure would lead him into trouble. But as he faced this reflection, he understood that adventure was part of who he was, and that he could balance his boldness with caution. He didn't have to choose between being brave and being careful—he could be both.

Coralia's mirror showed her as lost, adrift in a world that wasn't her own. It was a reflection of her fear that she didn't belong anywhere, that she was torn between the sea and the land. But as she looked deeper into the mirror, she realized that she didn't have to choose between the two worlds. She could belong to both, and that made her unique.

As they each faced their fears and insecurities, the mirrors began to shift. The distorted reflections faded, and the group saw themselves as whole and complete, each facet of their identity coming together to form a clear, unified reflection.

"We are many things," Lila said, her voice filled with understanding. "But all of those things make us who we are. We don't have to choose between them."

The group nodded in agreement, feeling a deep sense of acceptance and self-understanding. The mirrors had shown them that their identities were complex and multifaceted, but that was what made them strong.

As they left the maze of mirrors, they carried with them a newfound appreciation for the many facets of their identity. They had seen their strengths, their weaknesses, their fears, and their dreams, and they had learned that all of these parts were valuable.

The journey through the mirrors had taught them that they didn't have to be just one thing. They could be many things at once, and that was what made them unique.

Lessons Learned

1. **Identity is complex** – they realized that they were made up

of many different parts, each equally important.

2. **Embracing all facets of oneself** – by accepting both their strengths and weaknesses, they became more whole.
3. **Facing fears leads to growth** – the distorted mirrors showed them their fears, but by facing those fears, they grew stronger.
4. **We are not defined by one aspect of ourselves** – they learned that they didn't have to choose between different parts of their identity.
5. **Balance between strengths and weaknesses** – they understood that their strengths and weaknesses were both valuable and contributed to their identity.
6. **Self-reflection is powerful** – the mirrors taught them the importance of looking inward and understanding themselves.
7. **We are more than we appear** – their reflections showed them that they were more than just the surface version of themselves.
8. **Courage in vulnerability** – by confronting their fears and insecurities, they showed true courage.
9. **Unity through diversity** – their differences made them stronger, both as individuals and as a group.
10. **The journey of self-discovery** – the mirrors were a metaphor for their ongoing journey of self-discovery and growth.

Chapter 16: The Land of Whispers

As the group crossed into the Land of Whispers, a sudden hush fell over them. It wasn't just the quiet of an ordinary landscape, but a deep, palpable silence, as though the very air had stilled. The trees stood tall around them, their leaves barely rustling in the faint breeze. The sky was overcast, muted, with no birds singing, no insects buzzing. It was eerie, yet serene.

"What is this place?" Rafi asked, his voice seeming far too loud in the silence. His words echoed, then vanished into the stillness.

Ellie looked around, her brow furrowed. "I don't know, but it feels like we're supposed to listen."

The moment she said it, a strange sound met their ears—a faint murmur, barely audible. It was as if the world was full of whispers, voices too soft to make out clearly. They looked at one another, confused. The more they tried to speak loudly, the more their voices were swallowed up by the landscape. Only the softest words could be heard.

Coralia knelt down and placed her hand on the ground. "It's as if this place only responds to quiet. Shouting or even talking normally feels... out of place."

Zephyr, the strongest and most imposing of the group, attempted to roar, his voice usually commanding attention. But in the Land of Whispers, his powerful voice fell flat, fading before it could even travel. He shook his head, perplexed. "This place makes no sense. It's like the louder we try to speak, the less we're heard."

Ellie, always the quiet one, seemed oddly at peace. She whispered softly, "Maybe that's the point. Maybe this place isn't about being loud, but about listening."

The group paused, pondering her words. Slowly, they each lowered their voices, and with each whisper, the world around them seemed to come alive. The faint murmurs they had heard before became clearer, revealing themselves as conversations carried on the breeze. It was as though the land itself was speaking, but only to those who were willing to listen carefully.

"I think we're meant to hear something," Lila said softly, her voice barely above a whisper.

As they moved deeper into the Land of Whispers, they began to notice things they hadn't before. The soft rustling of leaves wasn't just the wind—it was a song, a quiet melody played by the trees. The faint hum in the air was a conversation between distant mountains. And the ground beneath their feet? It pulsed with the heartbeat of the earth, steady and rhythmic.

They walked in silence for some time, attuning themselves to the quiet world around them. It was as if the land was full of stories, but only those who listened carefully would be able to hear them.

After a while, they came upon a village nestled in the heart of the forest. The houses were small, made of stone and wood, with thatched roofs and narrow windows. The villagers moved about their daily lives in near silence, communicating with whispers and gestures.

A woman approached them, her expression kind but curious. She whispered, "Welcome, travelers. You are new to our land, I can see."

Rafi, still unused to the quiet, tried to speak, but his words were once again swallowed by the air. Frustrated, he lowered his voice to a whisper. "Yes. We're travelers. Can you tell us more about this place?"

The woman smiled. "This is the Land of Whispers, where only those who listen can truly understand. Here, the loudest voices are ignored, and only the softest are heard. We believe that true communication comes not from shouting to be heard, but from listening deeply to others."

Ellie's eyes lit up. "That's beautiful. It's so different from what we're used to."

The woman nodded. "In many places, the loudest voices drown out the quiet ones. But here, we value the whispers, the voices that often go unheard. We've learned that there is great wisdom in listening, in paying attention to what others have to say, even if they speak softly."

As the group explored the village, they noticed how the villagers moved and interacted. Every gesture was gentle, every word spoken softly. And yet, despite the quiet, there was a profound sense of connection among them. They communicated through looks, gestures, and soft words, each person taking the time to truly listen to those around them.

Lila, always in tune with the natural world, seemed to understand the village's way of life quickly. She whispered to the others, "This place is teaching us something important. It's showing us that we don't always need to be loud to be heard. Sometimes, the most important things are said quietly."

Rafi, who was often the most outgoing and exuberant of the group, struggled with the quiet at first. He was used to expressing himself boldly, and the restraint required here felt unnatural. But as the day wore on, he began to appreciate the value of quiet communication. He noticed things he hadn't before—the way people's eyes flickered with understanding, the subtle nods and smiles that conveyed entire conversations without a word.

Zephyr, who often took the lead in dangerous situations, found himself stepping back, letting the others guide the conversation. In the Land of Whispers, he realized that his strength wasn't needed. What was required here was patience, humility, and the willingness to listen.

As the group continued their journey through the village, they encountered a young girl sitting by a small stream. She was quietly weaving a garland of flowers, her fingers deft and nimble. The group approached her, curious about her silence.

"Why aren't you speaking?" Ellie whispered.

The girl looked up at them, her expression calm. "I don't need to speak to be heard," she whispered back. "If you listen closely, you'll hear what I'm saying."

The group exchanged confused looks, but they sat down beside her, watching as she continued to weave her garland. At first, the silence was uncomfortable, but as they sat there, they began to understand. The girl wasn't speaking with her voice, but with her actions. Every flower she wove into the garland had meaning—some were symbols of hope, others of love, and still others of peace.

Through her actions, the girl was communicating something far deeper than words could convey. She was showing them that sometimes, the most important messages are expressed not through what we say, but through what we do.

The group spent the rest of the day in the Land of Whispers, learning the value of quiet communication. They practiced speaking softly, listening intently, and paying attention to the unspoken messages around them. By the time the sun began to set, they had come to appreciate the beauty of the village's way of life.

As they prepared to leave, the woman who had first welcomed them approached. She whispered, "Remember what you've learned here. The loudest voices are not always the most important. Sometimes, it's the quiet ones that carry the greatest wisdom."

Lessons Learned

1. **The power of listening** – they learned that true understanding comes from listening deeply, not from speaking loudly.
2. **Quiet voices matter** – they realized that the quietest voices often have the most wisdom to share.
3. **Actions speak louder than words** – the girl by the stream showed them that sometimes actions can communicate more than words ever could.
4. **Patience in communication** – they discovered that communication isn't about rushing to be heard, but about taking the time to listen.

5. **Introversion is valuable** – the village taught them that being quiet and reflective is a strength, not a weakness.
6. **Connection through silence** – they experienced how silence can create a deeper connection than constant noise or conversation.
7. **Humility in communication** – Zephyr learned to step back and let others lead the conversation, understanding that communication isn't about dominance.
8. **Subtlety in expression** – the group realized that subtle gestures, looks, and touches can convey just as much as words.
9. **Respect for others' voices** – they came to appreciate the importance of respecting everyone's voice, no matter how softly they speak.
10. **Communication styles vary** – they learned that different people communicate in different ways, and that all styles are valuable.

Chapter 17: The Invisible Thread

The group walked along a winding path that cut through a dense forest, the trees towering overhead like ancient sentinels. The leaves whispered in the breeze, creating a soft, melodic rustling that felt almost like a lullaby. But despite the serenity of their surroundings, a sense of unease settled over the group. There was something about this forest—something that felt both familiar and unsettling at the same time.

"I can't shake the feeling that we're being watched," Coralia murmured, her eyes scanning the trees around them.

Lila nodded in agreement. "It feels like the forest is alive... and it's paying attention to us."

Zephyr, ever the protector, walked at the front of the group, his eyes sharp and vigilant. "Stay close. We don't know what's out there."

As they continued walking, the path began to narrow, twisting and turning in ways that seemed almost unnatural. The trees grew denser, their branches intertwining overhead to create a canopy that blocked out most of the sunlight. Shadows danced across the forest floor, and the air grew cooler.

Suddenly, without warning, the path split into several different directions, each one leading deeper into the forest. The group came to an abrupt stop, uncertainty flickering in their eyes.

"Which way do we go?" Rafi asked, his wings twitching nervously.

Before anyone could answer, the ground beneath their feet began to tremble, and the air shimmered with an unseen force. In an instant, the group was separated. One moment, they had been standing together, and the next, they were scattered along the different paths, each of them alone.

Ellie gasped, her heart pounding as she realized she could no longer see the others. "Rafi? Zephyr? Lila? Coralia?"

Her voice echoed in the empty forest, but no reply came. Panic began to rise in her chest, but she forced herself to stay calm. "Stay calm, Ellie. Think."

She closed her eyes and focused on her breathing, trying to steady the racing of her heart. As she stood there, alone in the forest, a strange sensation washed over her—a faint tugging, as if something invisible was pulling her forward.

"What...?" she whispered, her hand reaching out instinctively. She couldn't see it, but she could feel it—an invisible thread, pulling her in a specific direction.

Ellie's eyes widened as she realized what was happening. "The others. This thread... it's connecting us."

Without hesitation, she followed the pull of the invisible thread, trusting it to guide her through the twisting, turning paths of the forest. As she walked, the tugging grew stronger, and she felt a sense of reassurance wash over her. She wasn't alone. She was still connected to her friends, even though she couldn't see them.

Meanwhile, Rafi found himself in a similar situation. He stood on a narrow path, surrounded by towering trees, his wings fluttering anxiously. "Ellie? Zephyr? Anyone?"

But just like Ellie, his voice echoed through the empty forest, unanswered. Frustration welled up inside him, but before he could let panic take over, he felt it—a gentle tugging sensation, as if something was pulling him forward.

"What is this?" he muttered, reaching out to grasp at the air. His fingers closed around nothing, but the sensation remained. He could feel the invisible thread, connecting him to the others. It was faint, but it was there.

"I guess we're not as far apart as I thought," Rafi said with a relieved smile. He took a deep breath and began to follow the pull of the thread, trusting it to lead him back to his friends.

Zephyr, ever the protector, was wary of the invisible force pulling him forward. He didn't like the idea of something he couldn't see guiding him, but he knew better than to ignore his instincts. The thread felt familiar, like the bond he shared with the group, and though he couldn't see it, he could feel it tugging at him, urging him to move.

"This had better lead me to the others," he grumbled, following the pull with determined strides.

Coralia and Lila, both feeling the same invisible connection, also followed the thread. Though they couldn't see each other, they trusted the bond that tied them together. It was as if the thread represented their friendship, their trust in one another, and the strength of their shared journey.

As each of them followed the invisible thread, they navigated the winding paths of the forest with growing confidence. The forest, once unsettling and unfamiliar, began to feel less daunting. They knew they weren't alone, even if they couldn't see each other.

After what felt like hours of walking, the paths began to converge. One by one, they emerged from their separate trails and found themselves standing together once more in a small clearing. The relief on their faces was palpable as they rushed toward one another, embracing tightly.

"I knew we'd find each other," Ellie said, her voice filled with emotion. "I could feel the connection. I knew we weren't really apart."

Coralia and Lila nodded in agreement, their eyes bright with understanding. The invisible thread had shown them that their bond went deeper than physical proximity. It was a connection built on trust, friendship, and shared experiences.

As they stood together in the clearing, the invisible thread that had guided them through the forest seemed to fade away, no longer needed now that they were reunited. But the lesson it had taught them remained clear.

They had learned that even when separated, their connection to each other was unbreakable. It wasn't just the thread that had guided them—it was their trust in one another, their belief that they would always find their way back to each other.

Lessons Learned

1. **Trust in unseen connections** – the invisible thread represented their bond, showing that even when apart, they were still connected.
2. **Distance doesn't weaken bonds** – their physical separation didn't diminish their connection; it strengthened their trust in one another.
3. **Friendship is a lifeline** – the invisible thread was a metaphor for the support and trust that friends provide.
4. **Follow your instincts** – even though they couldn't see the thread, they trusted their instincts and followed its pull.
5. **Unity through trust** – the group's trust in each other allowed them to navigate the maze and reunite.
6. **Strength in togetherness** – the experience reminded them that they are stronger when they work together.
7. **Overcoming fear through connection** – the unsettling forest became less frightening once they trusted the bond between them.
8. **Belief in one another** – their belief that they would find each other again kept them moving forward.
9. **Invisible bonds are powerful** – the thread wasn't something they could see, but it was just as real and strong as any physical connection.
10. **Reconnection brings strength** – reuniting after being separated deepened their understanding of how much they rely on and support one another.

Chapter 18: The Dreamweaver's Tale

The sky above them darkened as the sun set, and the stars began to twinkle in the vast expanse of the night. The group found themselves in a quiet meadow, its grass soft and cool beneath their feet. Fireflies flickered in the air, casting a gentle glow across the landscape. There was something almost magical about the place, as if the air itself shimmered with the promise of dreams yet to come.

"I think we're meant to rest here tonight," Ellie said, her voice filled with a sense of calm. "The air feels different."

The others agreed, feeling the strange, dreamlike quality of the meadow settle over them. They made a small camp, and as they prepared to settle in for the night, a figure appeared on the horizon.

At first, the figure was barely visible, a mere shadow in the distance. But as it approached, the group realized that it was a tall, elegant being draped in flowing robes that seemed to shimmer like the night sky itself. The figure's eyes were gentle, filled with the wisdom of ages, and their movements were slow and graceful, as if they were floating rather than walking.

"Who are you?" Rafi asked, his voice soft with awe.

The figure smiled, their voice a melodic whisper. "I am the Dreamweaver, the keeper of dreams and the guide to the world of imagination. You are travelers, yes? You have come far on your journey."

The group nodded, feeling a deep sense of trust in the Dreamweaver's presence.

"You have learned much," the Dreamweaver continued, their voice flowing like a river of stars. "But there is still much to discover—within yourselves, and within each other."

The Dreamweaver gestured toward the meadow. "Tonight, I will guide you through the realm of dreams. You will enter one another's dreams and see the world through the eyes of your companions. You will learn their hopes, their fears, their deepest imaginings."

The group exchanged glances, excitement and curiosity filling their hearts.

"Are you ready?" the Dreamweaver asked.

They nodded in unison, eager to explore the dreams of their companions.

The Dreamweaver raised their hands, and a soft, shimmering mist began to rise from the ground. The air around them grew heavy with the scent of lavender and night-blooming flowers, and the stars above seemed to spin in slow, graceful circles.

One by one, the group drifted off to sleep, their bodies sinking into the soft grass as the Dreamweaver wove a delicate web of dreams around them.

Ellie was the first to enter the dream realm. She found herself standing in a vast, open ocean, the water calm and clear beneath her feet. But instead of feeling afraid, she felt at peace. The ocean was Rafi's dream, a reflection of his love for freedom and the endless possibilities of the sky.

In the dream, Rafi soared above the ocean, his wings wide and strong. He dipped and dived, playing with the wind and the waves, his laughter echoing across the water. Ellie watched with a smile, understanding for the first time just how deeply Rafi loved the feeling of flight. It wasn't just about adventure—it was about the pure joy of being free, of exploring the unknown.

Next, Rafi entered Lila's dream. He found himself in a dense, vibrant forest, the trees towering high above him. The air was filled with the sounds of birds and animals, and the forest itself seemed to pulse with life. Lila stood in the center of the forest, her hands gently touching the bark of a massive tree. She was calm, serene, her connection to nature deep and unbreakable.

Rafi watched in awe as Lila moved through the forest, her every step in harmony with the world around her. He had always admired her connection to nature, but seeing it in her dream made him realize just how profound that connection was. The forest wasn't just a place to her—it was a living, breathing entity, a part of her soul.

Lila, in turn, entered Coralia's dream. She found herself swimming through a vast, underwater world, the colors vibrant and alive. Coral reefs stretched out in every direction, teeming with life. Fish of every shape and size darted around her, and the water was warm and inviting. Coralia swam beside her, her movements graceful and fluid.

In Coralia's dream, the ocean was a place of wonder and beauty, but it was also a place of mystery. Lila could feel the pull of the deep, dark waters below, where unknown creatures lurked. Coralia wasn't afraid, though. She embraced the mystery, the unknown, finding peace in the depths.

Zephyr entered Ellie's dream next. He found himself standing on the edge of a cliff, the wind whipping around him. The sea stretched out below, wild and untamed, and the sky above was filled with storm clouds. Ellie stood beside him, her eyes fixed on the horizon.

In Ellie's dream, the storm wasn't something to be feared—it was something to be faced. Zephyr realized that Ellie's quiet strength came from her ability to weather the storms of life, to stand firm in the face of adversity. She wasn't loud or bold, but she was resilient, and that resilience was what gave her the power to keep going, no matter what challenges came her way.

Finally, Coralia entered Zephyr's dream. She found herself standing in the middle of a fierce storm, the wind howling and the rain pouring down in sheets. Zephyr stood tall and strong in the center of it all, his eyes glowing with determination. He wasn't afraid of the storm—in fact, he seemed to thrive in it. The storm was his domain, his strength.

In Zephyr's dream, the storm represented his power, but it also represented his responsibility. He had the strength to protect those he cared about, but that strength came with the burden of always being the one to stand against the storm. Coralia realized that while Zephyr was strong, he also carried the weight of that strength with him, and it wasn't always easy.

As the night wore on, the group continued to explore each other's dreams, learning more about their companions than they ever could have in the waking world. Each dream was a reflection of the dreamer's inner world—their hopes, their fears, their desires. And with each dream, the group's bond grew stronger.

When they finally awoke, the sky was just beginning to lighten with the first hints of dawn. The Dreamweaver stood before them, their eyes glowing softly in the early morning light.

"You have seen into the hearts of your companions," the Dreamweaver said, their voice filled with quiet wisdom. "You have learned their dreams, their fears, their hopes. And in doing so, you have grown closer, more connected."

The group nodded, still processing the depth of what they had experienced. The dreams had shown them parts of their companions that they had never known before, and it had deepened their understanding of one another in ways they hadn't thought possible.

"Thank you," Ellie said softly, her voice filled with gratitude. "We've learned so much from this."

The Dreamweaver smiled. "Remember what you have learned. Your dreams are a reflection of your inner selves, but they are also a bridge to understanding others. Never forget the power of imagination, the beauty of dreams, and the importance of seeing the world through the eyes of those around you."

With that, the Dreamweaver faded into the morning light, leaving the group to continue their journey with a newfound sense of connection and understanding.

Lessons Learned

1. **Dreams reveal inner truths** – they learned that dreams are a reflection of their deepest hopes, fears, and desires.

2. **Imagination bridges understanding** – by entering each other's dreams, they gained a deeper understanding of one another.
3. **Connection through creativity** – the dream world allowed them to connect in ways they couldn't in the waking world.
4. **Strength in vulnerability** – they saw the vulnerabilities of their companions, realizing that strength comes from acknowledging those fears.
5. **Embracing the unknown** – Coralia's dream taught them that the unknown can be a place of beauty and peace.
6. **Resilience in the face of adversity** – Ellie's dream showed them the power of quiet resilience in facing life's challenges.
7. **Power and responsibility** – Zephyr's dream revealed the weight of responsibility that comes with strength.
8. **Harmony with nature** – Lila's dream deepened their understanding of her connection to the natural world.
9. **The joy of freedom** – Rafi's dream showed them the pure joy he found in freedom and exploration.
10. **Shared dreams strengthen bonds** – by sharing their dreams, the group's bond grew stronger, built on mutual understanding and respect.

Chapter 19: The Festival of the Stars

The group walked into a valley that sparkled with the light of a thousand stars, not in the sky above them, but on the ground beneath their feet. It was as if the very earth had captured the stars and was now glowing with their light. The air was warm, filled with the scent of night-blooming flowers and the soft hum of distant music.

"What is this place?" Rafi asked, his eyes wide with wonder as he gazed at the glowing valley.

"It's like the stars have fallen to the earth," Coralia whispered, her voice full of awe.

A figure approached them from the far side of the valley, their robes shimmering with the same starlight that illuminated the ground. They carried a staff adorned with small, twinkling lights, and their face was kind and welcoming.

"Welcome, travelers, to the Festival of the Stars," the figure said, their voice melodic and soothing. "Tonight, we celebrate the stories of the stars—stories from every corner of the world, each one as unique as the star it represents."

The group exchanged excited glances. They had heard of festivals before, but nothing like this.

"The Festival of the Stars?" Lila asked, her voice filled with curiosity.

"Yes," the figure replied with a smile. "Every star in the sky represents a story, and tonight, we honor those stories by sharing our own. As each story is told, a new star is born, adding its light to the night sky. And when the festival is over, the stars will return to the heavens, carrying with them the stories of those who shared them."

The group was captivated by the idea. The thought of contributing their own stories to the night sky, to have them immortalized as stars, was both humbling and exhilarating.

"We'd love to be a part of this festival," Ellie said, her voice soft but eager.

The figure nodded. "Then come. Follow me, and I will show you where to add your stars."

They followed the figure through the glowing valley, marveling at the beauty of the stars beneath their feet. As they walked, they passed groups of people, each gathered around small fires, sharing their stories in hushed, reverent tones. With each story told, a new star seemed to rise from the ground and drift into the sky, joining the constellation that was slowly forming above.

The group was led to a small circle, where a fire flickered warmly in the center. The figure gestured for them to sit. "Each of you carries a story within you," they said. "And now is the time to share it. When you speak your story, a star will be born, and it will carry your words into the sky."

Ellie was the first to step forward. She took a deep breath and began to speak. "My story is one of quiet strength. I've always been the observer, watching from the sidelines, but through this journey, I've learned that my quietness is not a weakness. It's a strength. I don't need to be loud to make a difference. I've learned to stand firm in the face of challenges, to be resilient even when the storm rages."

As Ellie spoke, a soft glow began to rise from the ground, swirling around her before drifting into the sky. A new star appeared above, twinkling brightly as it took its place among the others.

Rafi stepped forward next, his wings fluttering slightly. "My story is about freedom," he said. "I've always been the one to rush ahead, to dive into the unknown without hesitation. But I've learned that freedom isn't just about flying fast or far. It's about knowing when to slow down, to take a moment and appreciate the world around you. It's about balance."

Once again, the ground glowed, and a new star rose into the sky, adding its light to the growing constellation.

Lila followed, her voice calm and steady as she spoke. "My story is one of connection. I've always felt a deep bond with the natural world, and through this journey, I've come to understand that connection even more. The earth, the trees, the animals—they're all part of something bigger, and so are we. We're all connected, and that connection gives us strength."

Another star rose into the sky, its light warm and golden.

Zephyr was next. His deep voice resonated through the valley as he spoke. "My story is about strength, but not just the kind of strength that comes from muscle or power. It's about the strength to be vulnerable, to admit when you need help, and to rely on those around you. True strength isn't about standing alone—it's about standing together."

A bright, shimmering star rose into the sky, joining the others in the constellation above.

Finally, Coralia stepped forward, her voice soft but sure. "My story is about belonging. I've always been a creature of the sea, but through this journey, I've learned that I can belong to more than one place. I can be of the ocean and of the land. I don't have to choose between them. I belong to both, and that makes me who I am."

The final star rose into the sky, completing the constellation. The group looked up in awe at the stars above them, each one representing their stories, their journeys, their growth.

As they sat together, watching the stars twinkle in the night sky, the figure who had guided them smiled. "Your stories are now part of the heavens," they said. "They will shine for all to see, a reminder of the journeys you have taken and the lessons you have learned."

The group sat in silence for a while, feeling the weight of their stories and the honor of having them immortalized in the stars. They had come so far on their journey, and now, their stories were part of something much bigger than themselves.

When the festival came to an end, and the stars began to return to the heavens, the group felt a deep sense of peace. They had shared their stories, and in doing so, they had added their light to the world. They had come together as individuals, but now, they were part of something greater—a constellation of stories, shining brightly in the night sky.

Lessons Learned

1. **Stories carry power** – their stories were immortalized in the stars, showing the lasting impact of sharing their experiences.
2. **Unity through individuality** – though each of their stories was unique, together they created something beautiful.
3. **Strength in vulnerability** – Zephyr's story showed them that true strength comes from admitting vulnerability and relying on others.
4. **Belonging is multifaceted** – Coralia's story reminded them that they could belong to more than one place, and that belonging is not limited to one identity.
5. **Connection to the natural world** – Lila's story reinforced the idea that everything is connected, both in nature and in their journey.
6. **Freedom through balance** – Rafi's story taught them that true freedom comes from balancing adventure with mindfulness.
7. **Quiet strength** – Ellie's story highlighted the power of quiet strength and resilience in the face of challenges.
8. **Shared experiences** – the Festival of the Stars showed them that sharing their stories brought them closer as a group.
9. **Immortality through stories** – their stories became part of the night sky, a symbol of their growth and journey.
10. **The beauty of diversity** – each star represented a unique story, but together they formed a beautiful constellation, illustrating the beauty of diversity in unity.

Chapter 20: The Circle of Trust

The landscape before them was different from anything they had encountered on their journey so far. The ground was barren, the sky a pale, washed-out blue, and the air was still and silent. There were no trees, no animals, no signs of life. It was as if they had stepped into a place devoid of everything they had come to expect from the world.

"This place feels... empty," Lila said, her voice filled with uncertainty.

Coralia nodded. "There's something off about it. It's like the world is waiting for something to happen."

As they walked deeper into the barren land, they came across a circle of large stones, each one placed equidistant from the next. In the center of the circle was a pedestal, and on the pedestal was a small, glowing sphere.

"What do you think that is?" Rafi asked, pointing to the sphere.

Zephyr stepped forward cautiously, his eyes narrowing as he studied the stone circle. "It looks like some kind of challenge."

Before anyone could respond, the air around them shimmered, and a voice echoed from all directions at once. "Welcome to the Circle of Trust. Here, you will be tested—not by strength or speed, but by your ability to trust one another."

The group looked at each other, confusion and curiosity mixing in their expressions.

"To complete the challenge," the voice continued, "you must rely on each other's strengths. Each of you possesses a unique ability, and only by working together will you succeed."

Rafi, always eager for a challenge, stepped forward. "I'm ready. What do we have to do?"

The ground beneath them began to shift, and the stones surrounding the circle glowed faintly. A series of obstacles appeared around the circle—walls too high to climb, deep pits too wide to jump, and narrow ledges that seemed impossible to cross.

"The obstacles before you cannot be overcome alone," the voice said. "But together, you can conquer them. Trust in one another's abilities, and you will succeed."

The group exchanged determined looks. They had faced countless challenges on their journey, but this one felt different. It wasn't just about using their individual strengths—it was about relying on each other, trusting that their companions could do what they couldn't.

Zephyr stepped forward first. "I'll go over the wall," he said, flexing his powerful muscles. "I can lift you up, but I'll need help getting down."

The group nodded, understanding what needed to be done. Zephyr approached the wall, his large frame making it easy for him to lift Ellie and Rafi over the top. Lila and Coralia followed, each of them trusting Zephyr's strength to get them over the obstacle.

Once they were on the other side, it was Ellie's turn to help. Using her quick thinking and agility, she found a way to lower a rope for Zephyr to climb down. Together, they had overcome the first obstacle, relying on Zephyr's strength and Ellie's resourcefulness.

The next obstacle was a wide pit, too far for anyone to jump across. Rafi, with his powerful wings, flew to the other side, but he knew that the others couldn't follow him.

"I can carry you across," Rafi said, looking at each of them in turn. "But you'll have to trust me."

Lila was the first to nod. "I trust you, Rafi. Let's do this."

One by one, Rafi flew them across the pit, his wings strong and steady. It wasn't easy—he had to make multiple trips, and the weight of his companions tested his endurance. But they trusted him, and that trust gave him the strength to carry them all safely to the other side.

The final obstacle was a narrow ledge that curved around a steep cliff. The ledge was barely wide enough for one person to walk on, and there was no room for mistakes.

Coralia, with her grace and balance, stepped forward. "I'll go first," she said. "Follow my lead, and I'll guide you through."

The group nodded, trusting Coralia's agility to lead them across the dangerous ledge. One by one, they followed her, their hearts pounding as they inched along the narrow path. Coralia's calm presence kept them steady, and her surefootedness gave them the confidence to keep going.

When they finally reached the other side, the group let out a collective sigh of relief. They had done it—together. Each of them had relied on the others, trusting in their unique abilities to overcome the obstacles.

As they stood together in the center of the circle, the glowing sphere on the pedestal began to pulse with light. The voice returned, calm and serene. "You have passed the test. You trusted one another, relied on each other's strengths, and overcame the challenges before you. The Circle of Trust has been completed."

The ground beneath them shifted once more, and the obstacles faded away, leaving the group standing in the now-empty stone circle. They had learned a valuable lesson—one that went beyond physical strength or individual abilities. They had learned that trust was the foundation of their success, and that by relying on one another, they could overcome any challenge.

As they prepared to leave the Circle of Trust, the group felt a renewed sense of confidence in their bond. They had always known that they were stronger together, but now they understood just how important trust was to their journey.

With the challenge behind them, they continued on their path, their hearts light with the knowledge that they could always rely on one another, no matter what obstacles lay ahead.

Lessons Learned

1. **Trust is the foundation of success** – they learned that trust in one another's abilities was the key to overcoming the obstacles.
2. **Each person has unique strengths** – by relying on each other's unique abilities, they were able to complete the challenge.
3. **Collaboration is essential** – they realized that working together was the only way to succeed.
4. **Strength isn't just physical** – they understood that mental and emotional strength were just as important as physical strength.
5. **Endurance through trust** – Rafi's ability to carry them across the pit was only possible because they trusted him.
6. **Leadership through calmness** – Coralia's calm and steady leadership guided them safely across the narrow ledge.
7. **Resourcefulness in problem-solving** – Ellie's quick thinking helped them find a way to lower Zephyr down the wall.
8. **Overcoming fear through trust** – by trusting one another, they were able to face their fears and take on the challenges.
9. **Support builds confidence** – knowing that they could rely on each other gave them the confidence to push through difficult obstacles.
10. **Unity in diversity** – their differences made them stronger as a group, allowing them to complement each other's abilities and work together as a cohesive team.

Chapter 21: The Song of the World Tree

As the group ventured deeper into the heart of the forest, the air seemed to grow thicker with an ancient, peaceful energy. The trees around them were massive, their roots intertwining like a vast network beneath the forest floor, and their branches reaching toward the sky as if they were attempting to touch the heavens. Yet, there was one tree that stood taller than all the others, its presence so powerful that it commanded the respect of everything in its vicinity. This was the World Tree.

The World Tree was unlike anything they had ever seen. Its trunk was as wide as a mountain, and its bark shimmered with colors that shifted between emerald green, deep gold, and soft silver. The roots seemed to pulse with a rhythmic hum, as though the very heartbeat of the earth resided within the tree. The leaves, which were the size of small canopies, fluttered in the wind, creating a melody so soft that it felt like a lullaby for the world itself.

"This... this must be the World Tree," Lila whispered in awe. Her deep connection with nature made her especially attuned to the tree's ancient presence, and she could feel its energy resonating within her.

"It's incredible," Ellie said, her voice barely a whisper. She reached out toward the bark, but something about the tree made her hesitate. It felt almost sacred, as though touching it without understanding its significance would be disrespectful.

As they stood there in awe, an ancient voice emerged from the tree itself, a voice so gentle yet powerful that it seemed to reverberate through the very fabric of their beings. "Welcome, travelers," the voice said. "You stand before the World Tree, the source of life, the embodiment of all that exists."

The group exchanged glances, each of them feeling the weight of the tree's words. "What is this place?" Rafi asked, his wings fluttering with curiosity.

"This is the heart of the world," the World Tree replied. "Each branch, each leaf, each root represents a different form of life, a unique expression of the universe. Though every part is different, all are connected. Without one, the others cannot thrive."

The group fell silent, absorbing the meaning of the tree's words. The vastness of its wisdom, the interconnectedness of all life—this was something far beyond what they had ever experienced.

"I can feel it," Lila said softly, her eyes closed as she placed her hand gently on the trunk of the World Tree. "It's like every living thing is connected. Every tree, every animal, every person. We're all part of the same whole."

Ellie stepped closer, nodding in agreement. "It's not just about being connected, though. It's about how our differences make the whole stronger. Each branch on this tree is different, but together they form something magnificent."

The World Tree's voice hummed with approval. "Yes, young one. Unity in diversity. Just as the branches of the tree are unique, so too are the beings that walk upon the earth. Each difference adds strength, beauty, and complexity to the whole."

Zephyr, ever the protector, approached the base of the tree. "But what happens when parts of the tree are weak or damaged? Does it harm the whole?"

The tree's deep voice resonated with wisdom. "In times of challenge, the stronger parts of the tree support those that are weakened. It is through this interconnectedness that all may thrive. The lesson here is not in removing the weak, but in understanding that we all support one another."

Rafi, his adventurous spirit always seeking new understanding, flew upward, gently landing on one of the lower branches of the World Tree. As he looked out, he could see the entirety of the forest stretched out before him, each tree a part of the vast network of life.

"The view from here is amazing," Rafi called down to the others. "It's like you can see how everything connects."

From where they stood on the ground, the others smiled. "Maybe that's the point," Coralia said thoughtfully. "From up there, you can see the big picture. Down here, we're all focused on our individual paths. But in the end, we're all part of the same journey."

The World Tree's branches swayed gently, as though acknowledging her words. "You have all seen the truth," the tree said. "The Song of the World Tree is the song of life itself. It is the song of unity through diversity, of strength through connection. Every living thing, no matter how small or different, contributes to the harmony of the world."

As the group listened to the World Tree's wisdom, they felt a deep sense of peace wash over them. They had learned so much on their journey, but this—this felt like the culmination of everything. The World Tree was a living symbol of everything they had come to understand: that differences were not weaknesses, but strengths, and that every being had a place in the grand tapestry of life.

The tree's voice grew softer, almost like a whisper carried on the wind. "Before you leave, remember this: You are all branches of the same tree. Though you are different, you are one. Nurture your differences, and in doing so, you will nurture the whole."

The group stood in silent reverence, each of them deeply moved by the experience. They had come to the heart of the world and learned one of life's greatest lessons: that unity does not mean sameness, but the celebration of diversity.

As they prepared to leave, they each took a moment to quietly thank the World Tree for its wisdom. Lila, especially, lingered for a while longer, feeling the deep connection between herself and the tree. It was as though her own roots were intertwined with the roots of the World Tree, and through that connection, she felt the heartbeat of the world itself.

When they finally turned to go, they carried with them a renewed sense of purpose. They knew that their journey was not just about discovering themselves, but about understanding how they fit into the greater whole. They were all branches of the same tree, and together, they would help the world thrive.

Lessons Learned

1. **Unity in diversity** – they learned that differences make the whole stronger, just as the branches of the World Tree each contribute to its beauty and strength.
2. **Interconnectedness of all life** – they realized that all living beings are connected, and that each part of the world is essential to the whole.
3. **Support in times of weakness** – they discovered that when one part of the whole is weak, the others must support it, reinforcing the importance of community and compassion.
4. **The value of differences** – the group understood that differences are not something to be feared or avoided, but celebrated and embraced.
5. **The big picture** – Rafi's view from the branches of the tree taught them that while they each have their own paths, they are all part of the same journey.
6. **Strength through connection** – the World Tree showed them that the strength of the world lies in its connections, and that no one is truly alone.
7. **Nurturing the whole** – they learned that by nurturing their own strengths and differences, they were also nurturing the world around them.
8. **The song of life** – the Song of the World Tree was a reminder that life itself is a harmony of different voices, and that each voice adds to the beauty of the whole.
9. **Embracing uniqueness** – they realized that being unique

does not mean being isolated, but rather contributing to the greater whole in a meaningful way.

10. **The wisdom of the earth** – the World Tree, as the heart of the earth, taught them that the earth itself holds deep wisdom, and that by listening to it, they could better understand themselves and the world around them.

Chapter 22: The Mask of the Moon

The night had fallen over the group as they continued their journey, the moon casting a soft, silvery light across the path ahead. It was a quiet, still night, the stars twinkling above them, and the gentle sound of the wind whispering through the trees. They had been walking for hours, their minds still filled with the lessons they had learned from the World Tree, when they stumbled upon something strange: a small stone altar, standing alone in the middle of a clearing.

On the altar lay five masks, each one shimmering in the moonlight. The masks were intricately crafted, with delicate designs etched into their surfaces. Each mask was unique, yet they all seemed to pulse with the same mysterious energy.

"What are these?" Rafi asked, stepping closer to examine the masks.

As if in response, a soft, melodic voice filled the air. "These are the Masks of the Moon," the voice said. "They are tools of reflection, of both hiding and revealing. Each mask allows you to choose what you show to the world, and what you keep hidden."

The group looked around, trying to find the source of the voice, but no one appeared. Instead, the masks seemed to glow brighter, as though beckoning them to come closer.

Ellie, always cautious, hesitated. "Should we... put them on?"

The voice answered gently. "The masks will not harm you. They will simply show you who you are, both on the outside and within. But beware—what you choose to hide may also reveal truths you have not yet faced."

Zephyr, ever the protector, stepped forward. "I'll go first," he said, picking up one of the masks. It was a strong, bold mask, with sharp lines and a design that seemed to represent power. As he placed it over his face, the mask molded to him perfectly, becoming an extension of himself.

For a moment, nothing seemed to happen. But then, as Zephyr looked at his reflection in a nearby pool of water, he saw something he hadn't expected. The mask had changed him—not physically, but in how he appeared to the world. It amplified his strength, making him seem even larger and more imposing than he already was. But it also hid something—his vulnerability, the part of him that longed to be seen as more than just a protector.

"This... this isn't all of me," Zephyr said quietly, removing the mask. "It shows my strength, but it hides my heart."

Ellie nodded, understanding. "The mask enhances the parts of ourselves that we want others to see, but it hides the parts we might not be ready to reveal."

One by one, the others took turns putting on the masks.

Rafi's mask made him appear more adventurous, more daring than ever before. His wings seemed larger, his presence bolder, but the mask also hid his moments of doubt, the times when he wasn't sure of himself.

Lila's mask amplified her connection to nature, making her seem almost ethereal, as though she was one with the earth itself. But it also hid her fear of being disconnected, of losing the bond she cherished so deeply.

Coralia's mask made her seem even more graceful and mysterious, her movements fluid like the ocean. But it hid her struggle to find balance between the sea and the land, between her two worlds.

Finally, Ellie put on her mask. It was simple, elegant, and it amplified her quiet strength, making her seem calm and composed. But it hid the deeper emotions she often kept locked away—the fear of being overlooked, the desire to be seen and heard for who she truly was.

As they stood together, each of them wearing their masks, they realized that while the masks allowed them to present a certain image to the world, they also concealed important parts of themselves.

"These masks... they're like the faces we show to the world every day," Ellie said quietly. "We all wear them, even if we don't realize it."

The voice returned, softer now. "Yes, that is the lesson of the Mask of the Moon. Every being wears a mask, whether they know it or not. Some masks are meant to protect, to hide vulnerabilities. Others are meant to enhance, to show strength. But true authenticity comes when you learn to balance what you reveal with what you keep hidden."

Zephyr removed his mask, his face thoughtful. "It's not about hiding who we are, but about understanding when to show certain parts of ourselves and when to keep others private."

Rafi nodded. "I always try to be brave and bold, but sometimes I'm scared. The mask let me hide that. But maybe I don't always need to hide it."

Coralia removed her mask and smiled softly. "It's about balance. Knowing when to show strength, and when to show vulnerability. We're all many things at once."

The group spent the rest of the night talking about the different masks they wore in their lives—the masks of bravery, of strength, of calm, of grace. They discussed how sometimes they used those masks to protect themselves, to hide their fears or insecurities. But they also realized that the masks weren't inherently bad. They were tools, ways of navigating the world.

"The real challenge," Ellie said, "is knowing when to take off the mask and let people see who you really are."

The voice of the Mask of the Moon spoke one final time before fading into the night. "Remember, the mask is not a lie, but a part of you. It is up to you to decide how much of yourself you reveal to the world, and how much you keep hidden. Balance is the key."

As the group prepared to leave the clearing, they left the masks on the altar, feeling lighter and more self-aware. They had learned that authenticity wasn't about revealing everything all the time—it was about choosing what to show and when, and understanding that their true selves were made up of many layers.

With the lesson of the Mask of the Moon behind them, they continued their journey, knowing that while they might still wear masks from time to time, they would do so with greater awareness and authenticity.

Lessons Learned

1. **We all wear masks** – they realized that everyone presents a certain version of themselves to the world, whether consciously or unconsciously.
2. **Balance between hiding and revealing** – they learned that authenticity is about finding the right balance between showing strength and vulnerability.
3. **Masks are tools, not lies** – the group understood that the masks they wore were not falsehoods, but parts of their true selves.
4. **The importance of vulnerability** – they discovered that it's okay to show their fears and insecurities, and that vulnerability is a strength.
5. **Understanding self-presentation** – they became more aware of how they present themselves to others, and how they can control that presentation.
6. **Authenticity is complex** – they learned that being authentic doesn't mean revealing everything at once, but choosing how and when to show different parts of themselves.
7. **Strength in vulnerability** – Zephyr realized that true strength comes not from hiding his vulnerabilities, but from embracing them.
8. **Fear of being seen** – Ellie faced her fear of being overlooked, and understood that showing her true self didn't mean she had to be loud.

9. **Bravery in admitting fear** – Rafi learned that being brave doesn't mean never being scared—it means being brave enough to admit it.
10. **Grace in balance** – Coralia discovered that her strength came from balancing the different aspects of her life, rather than hiding them behind a mask.

Chapter 23: The Heartbeat of the Mountain

The group stood at the base of a towering mountain, its peak hidden by the clouds. The air was crisp and cool, and the ground beneath their feet was rocky and uneven. The mountain seemed to pulse with a quiet, steady energy, as though it had a heartbeat of its own.

"We have to climb that?" Rafi asked, his wings fluttering nervously.

"Yes," Zephyr replied, his voice resolute. "But we'll do it together."

The mountain loomed before them, a daunting challenge that seemed almost impossible to overcome. But they had faced countless obstacles before, and they knew that this was just another test of their endurance and resilience.

"The Heartbeat of the Mountain," Lila said softly, as though she could feel the pulse of the earth beneath her. "It's alive, just like the World Tree."

Ellie nodded. "But this time, it's not about connection—it's about endurance. We're going to have to push ourselves."

With that, the group began their ascent. The path was steep and rocky, and the higher they climbed, the thinner the air became. Every step was a struggle, and each of them faced their own unique challenges as they made their way up the mountain.

Zephyr, with his powerful muscles, took the lead. His strength was an asset on the climb, but the altitude made it difficult for him to breathe. He had to pace himself, taking deep breaths and moving slowly. It was frustrating for him—he was used to being the strong one, the protector, and now he had to rely on his companions to help him when his strength wasn't enough.

Rafi, with his wings, was able to fly short distances, but the thin air made it hard for him to stay airborne for long. He had to land frequently, his wings trembling with the effort. It was a humbling experience for him—he was used to flying freely, but now he had to walk, just like the others.

Ellie, always the quiet observer, found herself struggling with the steep incline. Her legs ached, and the thin air made her dizzy. But she kept moving, one step at a time, her determination pushing her forward.

Lila, with her deep connection to the earth, felt the mountain's energy pulsing beneath her feet. It gave her strength, but it also weighed on her—she could feel the mountain's history, its age, and its power, and it was overwhelming at times. She had to remind herself to stay focused, to keep moving forward despite the weight of the mountain's presence.

Coralia, used to the fluidity of water, found the rigid terrain challenging. The rocky path felt unnatural to her, and she struggled to find her footing. But she was graceful, and she used that grace to navigate the uneven ground, moving with a quiet determination.

As they climbed higher, the group began to feel the strain of the journey. The air grew colder, the wind howled around them, and the path became narrower and more treacherous. But they kept going, each of them drawing on their own inner strength to push forward.

At one point, they came to a sheer rock face, too steep to climb without assistance. Zephyr, using his strength, helped the others scale the wall, one by one. But when it was his turn, he struggled. The altitude had drained his energy, and he couldn't pull himself up.

"I can't do it," Zephyr muttered, frustration evident in his voice.

"You don't have to do it alone," Ellie said softly, reaching down to help him. "We're in this together."

With Ellie's help, Zephyr managed to climb the wall. It was a humbling experience for him—he wasn't used to needing help. But he realized that endurance wasn't just about physical strength—it was about relying on others when you couldn't do it alone.

Further up the mountain, Rafi's wings gave out. He collapsed on the ground, gasping for air, his chest heaving with exhaustion. "I'm not used to this," he panted. "I'm not used to being grounded."

Coralia knelt beside him, her voice calm and soothing. "You're strong, Rafi. You've flown higher than any of us. But sometimes, even the strongest need to rest."

With Coralia's encouragement, Rafi found the strength to stand again. He knew he couldn't fly, but he could keep walking. And that was enough.

As they neared the summit, the group faced one final challenge: a narrow ledge that circled the peak, with a steep drop on either side. The wind howled around them, threatening to knock them off balance.

Lila, always in tune with the earth, went first. She moved slowly, carefully, feeling the mountain's heartbeat beneath her feet. The others followed, each of them focusing on their own steps, trusting the mountain to guide them.

When they finally reached the summit, they stood in awe of the view before them. The entire world seemed to stretch out beneath them, vast and beautiful. The sky was clear, the air crisp, and the heartbeat of the mountain pulsed beneath their feet, steady and strong.

"We did it," Ellie said, her voice filled with awe. "We made it to the top."

"Yes," Zephyr agreed, his voice quiet but proud. "But we didn't do it alone. We did it together."

The group stood in silence for a moment, each of them reflecting on the journey they had just completed. It had been difficult—perhaps the most difficult challenge they had faced yet—but they had made it. And they had learned that endurance wasn't just about pushing through physical obstacles. It was about resilience, about trusting in themselves and in each other.

As they began their descent, the heartbeat of the mountain continued to pulse beneath them, a reminder of the strength they had discovered within themselves. They had faced the challenges of the climb, and they had emerged stronger for it.

Lessons Learned

1. **Endurance is about resilience** – they learned that endurance isn't just about physical strength, but about mental and emotional resilience.
2. **Trust in others** – Zephyr realized that true strength comes from trusting in others when you can't do it alone.
3. **Pushing through limits** – Rafi discovered that even when he couldn't fly, he could still keep moving forward.
4. **Inner strength** – Ellie found her inner strength as she pushed through the physical challenges of the climb.
5. **Connection to the earth** – Lila's deep connection to the mountain gave her strength, but it also taught her to respect the weight of the world's history.
6. **Grace in adversity** – Coralia's grace allowed her to navigate the difficult terrain, but she also learned the importance of staying grounded.
7. **Support is essential** – they realized that they couldn't have made it to the top without supporting one another along the way.
8. **The journey is the challenge** – the group understood that the journey itself was the challenge, not just the destination.
9. **Humility in strength** – Zephyr's experience taught him the value of humility, and that even the strongest need help sometimes.
10. **The heartbeat of the world** – the mountain's heartbeat reminded them that they were part of something greater, and that their strength came from their connection to the world around them.

Chapter 24: The Gift of the Fireflies

As they made their way down the mountain, the group entered a dark, dense forest. The trees were tall and ancient, their branches intertwining to form a thick canopy that blocked out most of the light. The path ahead was shrouded in shadow, and the air was still and quiet, as though the forest itself was holding its breath.

"I can't see anything," Rafi muttered, his wings twitching nervously. "How are we supposed to find our way through this?"

"Stay close," Zephyr said, his voice calm but alert. "We'll find a way."

They walked in silence for a while, their footsteps muffled by the thick layer of leaves that covered the forest floor. The darkness pressed in around them, making it difficult to see more than a few feet ahead. It was unsettling, and each of them felt the weight of the shadows, as though the forest was hiding something.

Just when they were beginning to lose hope, a soft light appeared in the distance. It was faint at first, just a flicker in the darkness, but as they got closer, they realized that it was a firefly—its tiny body glowing brightly in the shadows.

"Look," Lila whispered, her voice filled with wonder. "A firefly."

The firefly hovered in the air for a moment, then darted ahead, its light guiding the way. Without a word, the group followed.

As they walked, more fireflies appeared, their small lights flickering in the darkness. Soon, the entire forest was filled with the soft glow of hundreds of fireflies, their lights dancing in the air like tiny stars.

"It's beautiful," Coralia said softly, her eyes wide with awe.

The fireflies led them deeper into the forest, their lights illuminating the path ahead. It was still dark, but the presence of the fireflies made it feel less oppressive. The group walked in silence, their hearts lifted by the gentle glow of the tiny creatures.

After a while, they came to a small clearing. The fireflies gathered around them, their lights forming a glowing circle in the darkness.

"What do you think they want us to do?" Ellie asked, her voice quiet.

"I think they're showing us that even the smallest lights can make a difference," Lila said thoughtfully. "The forest was so dark, but these tiny fireflies have guided us through it."

Rafi nodded. "It's like each firefly's light is small on its own, but together, they create something powerful."

The group stood in the clearing, watching as the fireflies continued to dance around them. There was something comforting about the tiny creatures, something that reminded them of the power of small acts of kindness, of how even the smallest contributions could make the world a brighter place.

"They're teaching us something important," Zephyr said quietly. "That no matter how small we feel, no matter how insignificant our actions may seem, we all have the power to make a difference."

The fireflies' lights pulsed softly, as though they were agreeing with his words. The group stood in silence, each of them reflecting on the lesson they had just learned.

As they prepared to leave the clearing, the fireflies began to drift away, their lights fading into the darkness. But the lesson they had taught remained with the group: that even the smallest light can shine brightly in the darkest of places.

Lessons Learned

1. **Small acts of kindness matter** – the fireflies taught them that even the smallest actions can make a big difference.
2. **The power of community** – the group learned that when individuals come together, their combined efforts can create something powerful.
3. **Light in the darkness** – the fireflies reminded them that

even in the darkest times, there is always hope and light to be found.

4. **Everyone has something to contribute** – they realized that no matter how small or insignificant they might feel, they each had something valuable to offer.
5. **The beauty of small things** – the fireflies showed them that sometimes, it's the smallest things that bring the most joy and wonder.
6. **Guidance in unexpected places** – they discovered that help and guidance can come from the most unexpected sources.
7. **Hope in the midst of challenge** – the fireflies' lights lifted their spirits, showing them that hope is always present, even in difficult times.
8. **Unity through small efforts** – the group understood that when everyone contributes, no matter how small, the result is greater than the sum of its parts.
9. **The power of presence** – the fireflies' presence reminded them that sometimes, just being there for someone can be enough to make a difference.
10. **Light and darkness coexist** – they learned that light and darkness are both part of life, and that even in the darkest moments, there is always a light to guide the way.

Chapter 25: The Symphony of Us

As the group made their way back to Harmony Hill, they couldn't help but reflect on everything they had learned throughout their journey. They had traveled to distant lands, met incredible beings, and faced challenges that had tested their strength, resilience, and understanding of the world. But now, they were returning to the place where it had all begun.

Harmony Hill was just as they remembered it, with its rolling green fields, gentle breezes, and the familiar feeling of magic in the air. But something was different this time. It wasn't the place that had changed—it was them.

"We've come full circle," Ellie said softly as they stood at the top of the hill, looking out over the landscape.

"Yes," Lila agreed, her voice filled with a quiet sense of awe. "But we're not the same people we were when we started this journey."

Zephyr nodded. "We've learned so much. About ourselves, about each other, about the world. And now it's time to bring it all together."

As if in response to his words, a soft, melodic sound filled the air. It was faint at first, but as they listened, the sound grew louder and more complex, like a symphony being played by invisible musicians.

"What's that?" Rafi asked, his ears twitching as he listened to the music.

"It's the Symphony of Us," a voice said, echoing through the air. The group turned to see the figure of an elderly woman standing at the base of the hill. She was dressed in robes that shimmered with the colors of the rainbow, and her eyes sparkled with wisdom.

"The Symphony of Us?" Coralia repeated, her voice filled with curiosity.

The woman nodded. "Yes. The Symphony of Us is the culmination of everything you have learned. It is the harmony that comes from embracing your differences, from understanding that each of you brings something unique to the world."

The group exchanged glances, understanding dawning on their faces.

"The Symphony of Us is not just a song," the woman continued. "It is a reflection of who you are, as individuals and as a group. Each of you has a unique melody, a special contribution to the symphony. And when you come together, those melodies create something beautiful, something greater than any one of you could create alone."

The group stood in silence, each of them absorbing the meaning of her words. They had spent so much time discovering themselves and each other, and now they realized that everything they had learned had been leading to this moment.

"You are all part of the symphony," the woman said gently. "Now, it is time to play your part."

One by one, the group stepped forward, each of them adding their unique voice to the symphony.

Ellie's melody was soft and steady, like a river flowing gently through a forest. It carried with it the strength of quiet resilience, the power of standing firm in the face of adversity.

Rafi's melody was bold and adventurous, like the wind rushing through the sky. It was filled with the joy of freedom, the thrill of exploration, and the courage to face the unknown.

Lila's melody was earthy and grounded, like the roots of a tree reaching deep into the soil. It was a reflection of her connection to the natural world, of her understanding that everything is connected.

Zephyr's melody was powerful and steady, like the beat of a drum. It carried with it the strength of protection, the responsibility of leadership, and the willingness to be vulnerable.

Coralia's melody was fluid and graceful, like the ebb and flow of the ocean's tides. It was a reminder of the balance she had found between the sea and the land, between her two worlds.

As each of them played their part, the symphony grew richer, more complex, and more beautiful. The melodies intertwined, creating a harmony that was greater than the sum of its parts.

The woman smiled as she listened to the music, her eyes filled with pride. "This is the Symphony of Us," she said softly. "A celebration of diversity, of unity, of the beauty that comes from embracing who you are and sharing it with the world."

The group looked out over Harmony Hill, knowing that their journey was far from over. They had learned so much, but there was still more to discover, more to share, more to create.

Lessons Learned

1. **Harmony through diversity** – they learned that true harmony comes from embracing their differences and working together.
2. **The power of unity** – the Symphony of Us showed them that when individuals come together, they create something greater than the sum of their parts.
3. **Celebrating uniqueness** – they understood that each of them had a unique contribution to make, and that their individuality was what made the symphony beautiful.
4. **Strength in collaboration** – the symphony reminded them that they are stronger when they work together and support one another.
5. **The journey is ongoing** – they realized that while they had learned a lot, their journey of discovery and growth was far from over.
6. **Every voice matters** – each of their melodies was important, and together, they created something truly extraordinary.
7. **The beauty of differences** – they learned that differences are not something to be feared, but something to be celebrated.
8. **Resilience in the face of challenges** – the Symphony of Us

reflected their strength and resilience, their ability to overcome challenges together.

9. **Connection through music** – the symphony showed them that music, like life, is a reflection of the connections we make with others.
10. **The power of contribution** – they realized that by sharing their unique talents and strengths, they could make the world a brighter, more harmonious place.

Don't miss out!

Visit the website below and you can sign up to receive emails whenever Victoria Bennett publishes a new book. There's no charge and no obligation.

https://books2read.com/r/B-A-WBILC-XKUDF

BOOKS 2 READ

Connecting independent readers to independent writers.

The Good Child

Inspiring values and fellowship

About the Publisher

The Good Child Academy is a premier publisher dedicated to creating enchanting and educational children's books that inspire imagination and creativity. With a focus on delivering high-quality stories, the academy collaborates with talented authors and illustrators to produce books that captivate young minds. Specializing in themes like adventure, learning, and seasonal celebrations such as Halloween, Good Child Academy ensures that each book fosters curiosity, empathy, and a love for reading. Their mission is to nurture the next generation of lifelong readers.

Read more at https://www.patreon.com/thegoodchild/shop.

Milton Keynes UK
Ingram Content Group UK Ltd.
UKHW022232051124
450708UK00014B/1011

9 798227 961297